The Survivor of the Edmund Fitzgerald | Joan Skelton

Penumbra Press | Manotick, ON | 2007

A portion of Nordri's dialogue was
excerpted from the award-winning article
"Bushwoman," published in *Lake Superior
Magazine*, July 1998 (lakesuperior.com).

Cover photo by Joan Skelton

PENUMBRA PRESS, *publishers*
Box 940 | Manotick, ON | Canada
K4M 1A8 | penumbrapress.ca

Printed & bound in Canada

Penumbra Press gratefully acknowledges
the financial support of the Government of
Canada through the Book Publishing
Industry Development Program (BPIDP)
for our publishing activities. We also
acknowledge the Government of Ontario
through the Ontario Media Development
Corporation's Ontario Book Initiative.

*Library and Archives Canada
Cataloguing-in-Publication Data*

Skelton, Joan
    The survivor of the Edmund Fitzgerald/
    Joan Skelton — 2nd ed.
    ISBN 978-1-897323-11-3
    1. Shipwrecks —
    Superior, Lake — Fiction.
    2. Edmund Fitzgerald (Ship) — Fiction.
    I. Title.
PS8587.K44S97 2007   C813'.54
    C2007-906826-X

To every Clara….

But in the frost of the dawn,
Up from the life below,
Rose a column of breath
Through a long cleft in the snow

DUNCAN CAMPBELL SCOTT, *The Forsaken*

Intruders

CLARISSA SNAPPED OPEN the padlock on the gate and drove her car through. She locked the gate behind her and took a deep breath as she got back into the car. Tasha, the family German shepherd beside her, demonstrated an excitement that Clarissa's deliberate, slow movements did not.

I have to face up to this. And, as a Wheatley, naturally I have to do it alone. If only....

The flaming maples arching over the narrow road distracted her. She had never seen the Algoma forest so beautiful. The graceful greens were bewitched into reds, oranges, umber, and yellow, with whirling arrows of black spruce and waltzing boughs of pine adding a *cloisonné* outline to the colours. Clarissa rolled down the car window and absorbed the crisp fall air.

The road was narrow, hilly, and deserted. It was unlikely any of the other cottagers would be here.

Campers, not cottagers, if you want to use the lingo of the area. Mother refused. I guess so do I. Sounds like you're a Boy Scout.

What would it matter, anyway, if other cottagers were around? The subdivision was deliberately planned for privacy, with huge twenty- to hundred-acre lots, no phones, no hydro, and certainly no social organization. No clustering together in the garrison mentality here.

'*Aren't you afraid of bears?*'

'*I've got a pepper spray.*'

'*What about being alone?*'

'*You mean without a man for protection?*'

'*Yes.*'

'*Must I be reduced to dependency?*'

'*I hope you'll take Tasha.*'

'*I am.*'

'*There's a shotgun hidden under the floorboards, you know. Under the armoire.*'

'*I know. I'm taking the shells.*'

Although the Wheatleys always left a twelve-gauge shotgun at the cottage for protection, they never left the shells there, even if they went away for a day. They had no intention of providing ammunition should their gun fall into the wrong hands.

With a culture gradually being based on violence, yet a disproportionate reduction in police protection, survival was coming to depend on the wile of a frontier mentality. Of concern also was another adversely educated animal, the "garbage bear," its natural isolationist instincts corrupted by human contact.

'*You've got guts.*'

'*I'm not going to let fear keep me away from something I love.*'

I'm surprised I said that. I am surprised to realize I love that place.

It wasn't the spectre of victimization that was bothering her as she manoeuvred the car over the bald outcrops of lava and slithering screes of shale.

It's the fear of facing Mother.

She drove up a steep basaltic eruption, trying to offset the wheels away from the ruts worn in the shallow overburden.

'*Watch it!*'

'*Fuck!*'

'Don't be unladylike, Clarissa.'

Oh, gawd.

It's so wretchedly easy to bottom out if you aren't careful.

Just over a rise, Clarissa turned down the road to the Wheatley cottage at the GULL ROCK sign. She jounced and bounced to the waterfront.

'I always hold my breath as I drive into the clearing for the cottage. Maybe intruders. Maybe vandalism. Maybe a tree down. Maybe the animals reclaiming their space.'

Moth-er! Keep out of my mind.

Even before Clarissa shut off the ignition, her thoughts were engulfed by sound. It pulsed through her body. Even before unlocking the cottage, she and the dog ran to a high outcrop of lava overlooking the shore. It cascaded with bonsai pine. From this vantage point, she watched the blue-green waves of Lake Superior billowing into avalanches of foam.

What a wonderful wind.

'Marvellous.'

Mother always said that: 'marvellous.'

Gusts of a north crosswind whipped across the crest of the breakers and she saw the waves create the Ojibwa manitou, the sea lynx, Mishipishu. It rose up and submerged into the turbulent Lake.

It was the first time Clarissa had seen this phenomenon.

"He runs against the prevailing waves," her mother had said.

Naturally, Mother would think of a god as a he, as the human race as man. What do you expect? Society had indoctrinated her.

"Come on, Tasha. Let's get to work."

'Make a wish, Clarissa. You saw Mishipishu. Your wish will be granted.'

Fergawdsakes, Mother.

Clarissa unlocked the door and most of the shutters of the cottage. She left the low, easily accessible windows shuttered, even if it meant losing some view.

Propping open the door, she began to unpack the car, hanging food bags over her wrists, purse over her shoulder, carrying a heavy cooler with two hands.

Got to get the fridge and stove lit. Don't know if I'll bother with the generator, the propane lights'll do for today.

Once inside the door, she stopped, transfixed.

The Eastlake table, the antique rocking chair, the old photos on the wall, gawd, the smell of baking bread, the skylights she'd insisted on having, the mousetraps set before leaving, no mice, she was everywhere. She! Mother! This was her domain, her love, her place, it's already begun smothering me, dominating me, like she....

Get going, you can't just stand here with the door and your mouth open.

The unpacking and settling-in pre-empted her underlying layer of thoughts. The car was unpacked, the propane fridge and stove lit, and the food put away. Her luggage was taken upstairs, her purse hung on the back of a chair. She put her laptop on the Eastlake table and realized she needed to go out to the loo.

The pepper spray. Always hang the holster over your shoulder. So easy to hang over your shoulder. Haven't had time to check for bear sign.

And take off your watch, function on natural time, bed with the sun, up with the sun.

Just like Mother did.

Will I ever escape her?

Lighting the big airtight stove was next. Fortunately there was kindling and firewood piled under the cottage, although she would have to collect more kindling from the beach. She didn't trust her ability to keep the fire going; it would probably have to be re-lit in the morning. She unfolded her sleeping bag and draped it over a chair near the fire.

Where's that gun? Where did Andrew say it was hidden? Not in the locked gun cupboard. Too obvious. Too easily vandalized. Underneath the armoire?

She took the gun to the dining room table. She unpacked the

cosmetic case that carried, and camouflaged, the shotgun shells. Checking the gun to make sure the safety was on, she flinched as she pressed the button that snapped the chamber closed and allowed her to insert two shells underneath into the reserve chamber. What was it really called? The magazine tube? She didn't know or care about the names of the gun's parts, but she had insisted her father teach her how to handle one.

Mother never learned. Depended on everybody for everything. She dominated everybody with her dependency, couldn't stay alone here, got so fat she couldn't cut her toenails, couldn't put out the garbage. According to Margaret Atwood's poem, this 'help me' was, in fact, the real siren's song.

In those days, could she have dominated with independence? Gawd, what respect, what power, did she have … as a housewife?

'Do you work?'

'No. I'm a housewife.'

How often had I heard that? She worked her butt off yet society didn't regard it as work. Worse, nor did she. No wonder she sang the siren's song.

All that drudge, screaming kids, endless cooking.

Important, when you think about it.

Balance needed, though.

Clarissa pulled back the stiff lever that opened the chamber in the barrel and inserted another shell, three shells in all, the legal number. A plug had been inserted into the magazine tube to prevent using five shells, the number the gun was made for. What kind of tokenism was this with all the high-powered automatic weapons that were legal, Clarissa had asked.

Yes. I remember how to load this thing all right.

Better unload it.

'Never leave a gun loaded.'

Yes, Mother.

Am I stupid to unload it? With the chamber open, it's got two safeties.

Be responsible. Unload it.

She took the shells out of the gun, careful not to jam it. She hung the gun on the rack in the special cupboard behind the guest-bedroom door. The cosmetic case of shells was put in a dresser drawer. She left the case open.

Water. I have to get water.

Down the stairs to the beach and across to the shore, the dog with a stick in its mouth ran around latticing the rippled sand with its tracks. The outcrops of red lava were more exposed than she had ever seen them, the shoreline entirely changed because of a low water level. It could be a *seiche*, the slow-motion sloshing back and forth of water in a big lake. Maybe it was the subtle process of the north shore of Lake Superior still springing back from the weight of the last glacier, gradually tipping it like a saucer southward. Worse, and not subtle, was the gradual evaporation of the Lake. Or drainage.

"Where would we be without water, Tasha?"

She watched the waves and gauged their rhythm, then quickly as they subsided dipped one pail at a time into potholes in the lava that provided natural water holes at the edge of the Lake.

The capitalized word "Lake" printed itself out in her mind. The capitalization of the first letter signified not only a short form for Lake Superior, like the Hat for Medicine Hat, the capitalization implied much more. It bespoke a covenant among northerners of reverence and importance and respect.

Especially for Mother.

'All words are metaphors.'

Yes, Mother.

Clarissa turned around and walked towards the cottage, her hair whipping across her face. The cottage was barely visible, stained brown with a brown roof, trees so close they hugged it.

'Don't remove one single more tree,' I can hear Mother saying as it was being built, the trees so close they whispered against the cottage in a wind.

'How can we justify wantonly killing trees while condemning South Americans for doing the same?'

Just like Mother.

Clarissa prepared a simple dinner. Wearing her parka and a hat, she ate on the deck outside the bedroom upstairs. No wine. She wanted her reaction time as fast as possible. Her mother never sat up here because there was no sun protection. Consequently, Clarissa felt comfortable.

My space.

Through the balletic limbs of the red pine she watched a few remnants of the once-ebullient gull colony huddling on Gull Rock, its orange lichen contrasting against the white-streaked blue of the Lake and sky.

What was that? Over the roar of the waves, a high-pitched hocus-pocus cry announced itself in the trees. Where is it? There, a pileated woodpecker, like a relict of the past, an effigy of a pterodactyl, no, an avian magician, flying through the woods, its jaunty red cap, triangular face and white-lined cape of black wings, so fitting in the magic of this place that she was fighting so hard to resist.

Sunset. A miracle of light. It bathed her as she collected the curly-cues of driftwood on the beach for kindling. Some she saved in a pile by the shore, Rorschach shapes she could not bear to burn. As she collected, she gradually veered northward on the shore.

The Edmund Fitzgerald sank just out there, to the northwest. The whole crew of twenty-nine men were lost. An unaccounted-for body was found on the bottom of the Lake outside the broken hulk.

Don't even think about walking the other way, southward, to where she....

§§§

Night. Blackness. Lack of sound. The roar of the Lake gradually diminishing since sundown. The house locked up tight. The sleeping bag warm and cuddly. The dog on the rug beside her bed, its alert senses her intruder alarm.

The turbulent weather made her feel more secure. The bad types were not likely to brave it.

Up at dawn, her thoughts about what to do were immediately dispelled by a look out the window. Snow! The yellows and reds of the trees were frosted with white, their shapes elongated and slimmed by its weight into Modigliani sculptures.

You're using Mother's art metaphors.

"Look at that sun, Tasha. The Lake's so calm. Shimmering blue, green, white from the sand, red from the lava. Get your ball. We'll breakfast later. See the Lake later."

Heading up the driveway, she and the dog exulted in the snow-capped flaming colour of the forest.

Whoever has seen anything so magnificent, so unusual?

This is mine.

Not Mother's.

On the main cottage road, now a tunnel, no, a bower, of colour, she noticed tracks.

What?

Who?

Human?

"Tasha, they're drilled into the snow single file, a line.... I can't tell what.... It's got to be a wolf. Or wolves. No human could walk under a low branch like that. The tracks are too big and deep for fox."

She was thrilled. Might she actually hear wolves howling in the wild? Live? Maybe she and Tasha would call them.

When the dog was young, Clarissa, with the help of recordings and her own howling, holding the dog firmly and close to her face, had taught Tasha — urged her, teased her, really — to recapture her howling instincts. Because of the dog's good nutrition and manipulated breeding for heavy bones, especially the chest, she had an almost operatic contralto voice, rich and mellifluous, but always reluctant. You could tell she regarded howling as a regression. She seemed almost embarrassed.

"It's part of you. Don't be ashamed of it," Clarissa had said.

As they gamboled along the road, she and the dog were exhilarated by the technicolour forest. They became part of it.

"Wait a minute, Tasha. There's smoke coming out of the place that's been for sale for ages."

"Hall-o. You out valking, too, missus?"

There, around a crook in the narrow road that Clarissa knew led to an old, broken-down cottage came an old woman, an old, old woman. She was in a long, billowing dress, down jacket, and work boots. Her fine, white hair was gathered at the nape of her neck in a ponytail. She was using a heavy walking stick made from a straight, de-barked limb.

"I valking, too. It very beautiful today."

'Marvellous.'

"Yes, it is. But who are you?"

"I Nordri Karjalainen."

"Ah, Mrs. Kar...."

"Yus call me Nordri. But come on, come on down with me to camp and I get you good cuppa coffee."

"That would be nice. I came out before I had breakfast."

"And good coffee cake, too, *pulla*, Finnish coffee cake. What's yur name?"

"I'm Clarissa Wheatley. Our cottage is GULL ROCK."

"I see dat GULL ROCK sign on de road."

In the small, warm cabin that had been painted and cleaned up, the rough logs without a hint of dust, the beige linoleum floor spotless, the two intergenerational women sat and talked.

Clarissa learned that Nordri had bought the little cottage on the shore of Lake Superior as an ascension toward God and death and spirituality and peace, although she did not use those words.

"I need to be part of something good again, the trees and birds and animals and water. I want breathe clean air.

"When young, I live long time in bush with husband who bush-whacker. I raise my little kiddies. I happy dere. I am vorking yus like man. I learn how to use cross-cut saw. Mine husband makes doze kiddies little saw or *poka saha*, which maybe how Pukaskwa got name, I am not for sure.

"Some peoples say Pukaskwa rhymes with swear word that bushwhackers use when cutting with saw not sharp. Word begins with F. Put F at beginning of Pukaskwa instead of P. I never say dat bad word. Not once in whole life.

"Matti die. I leave bush. I raise dose kids alone in city."

"How did you ever do it?"

"I not say. I coming here to escape bad things. Lotsa bad things. I don't vant leave dis worl and not feel again little bit what is good.

"I come here, to … to … how can I say? … to get dat good."

"When are you going back?"

"I not for sure."

"More snow will come soon."

"I have skis. But you, missus, why you here?"

"I just needed a break."

Liar.

"I have a high-stress job."

Who doesn't?

"I am very busy."

Who isn't? It's a badge of importance!

"What you do?"

"I'm an accountant."

"Long way from dat here. You coming lotsa time alone?"

"Ah, no … actually, this is the first time…. I haven't been here for … gee, it must be a couple of years, no several, actually many … ah … not since…."

"You scared?"

"A bit. But I like it here."

Liar.

"Hard to fool self when alone in front of dat big Lake."

'Time to face up,' my therapist said.

"I climb up on dat high point out dere, I stretch my arms to de sky, and I feel myself move into dat sky, into the wind, de barriers gone, I feel, what kinda thing I wanta say, I feel … a new dimension? Is dat word right? You understand?"

"I'm not sure. But I have to go now. Thanks so much for the delicious coffee and bread. *Pulla.*"

"Yur welcome. But don't go, missus. I never get time to talk. Stay little bit more. I not talk so good. I know dat. Sometimes pretty good. Sometimes terrible. Sometimes words right. Sometimes wrong. Getting worse as getting older. But I like to talk."

"I really must get back."

"Nobody knows how hard it was for homesteader. My parents homesteaders outside what is now Thunder Bay. Hard for me, hard for them. But work is good. I never mind.

"Most of time we have lots to eat, what we grow on farm, and what we gather. There lotsa berries and Labrador tea, and sometimes getting moose or wild rice from Indians, sometimes even maple syrup from those Indians on Mount McKay who only ones having hardwood maple around this place."

Gawd, how older people go on.

"Nordri, I really must go.…"

"Alla time gun loaded by door. Everybody learn shoot, even my mother, even kids, and if rabbit run by, it get shot. After, when everybody can buy meat, Pa-Pa say he never understand why mans kill for fun of it.

"We always clean. Saw-oo-na is alla time hot, either drying clothes or vegetables, or ready for us to jump into steaming washtub of water. I gather water from well, sometimes Lake. Lotsa times my legs freeze. No girls or womans wear trousers then. Just dresses. So cold on legs. Women not liberated then. Women not liberated now, either."

"Now, Nordri, just a minute. What about…"

"Life pretty good on that farm. Maybe eighty-five frost-free days. Or so government say. My fadder not believe. We choose crops carefully and they grow like jungle because days so long. Lotsa trees to clear, stumps to burn, lotsa rock in this place. But there is always Lake — Lake Superior — with its 'harvest' of fish. He use that big word, harvest. And, alla time Pa-Pa say: 'Praise be the Lake.'

"He say it often, when he catch fish, when he drink water, it so clear, so wonderful to drink. He try to say it good, like Englis. He know must talk Englis to get ahead. We forbidden speak Finn.

"When I small and nobody to play with except make-believe kids, I creep down to Lake and watch those peoples, those Indians, today called natives or first peoples or aboriginals. They come so quiet in birch-bark canoes and make wigwams on sand. Soon I make friends with those kids. I learn they call themselves Anishinabe, first peoples. Sometimes they called Ojibwa because they wear moccasins with puckered seams. I had friend, O-shaw-gus-co-day-way-qua. I called her O-shaw-gus. Her name mean 'daughter of the green mountain.' That name right for her, for her people, too.

"She show me how play *napowagon*, some kinda game with little bunch of spruce bows and pointed stick. We make it lotsa times, cutting spruce boughs and winding tight with sinew, leaving long piece sinew to tie on pointed stick. When stick good and sharp from knife, we are swinging bough up in air and catching it on stick. Not easy. But gets easier as work at it."

"This is interesting, Nordri, but…."

"Those peoples always share, giving me smoked fish and bannock. I am always trying to get my mudder make bannock, it taste so good. When I grow big, I make it; but never taste as good.

"Those peoples treat whole world like it family. Even though killing animals, they say those animals not stay dead if kill nice. If killing bad, or maybe killing too many or killing cruel, they say those animals never come back and Anishinabe is stalked by Windigo, spirit of starvation.

"When I start to school builded by all those mans from farms around us, those kids call my friends 'savages.'

"Pretty soon I see them no more. They told to go to some kinda place on mountain, now called Mount McKay. They not supposed to wander no more, no more.

"Even though I justa kid I wonder how they live inside small place, small for them, when they used to hunting and fishing and gathering food all over place.

"When Matti and I marry we go into bush. We speak Finn alla time. Matti a bushwhacker."

"Nordri. Thanks so much for everything. I have to go. I have to get back."

You said those same words to Mother the last time you saw her.

Walking back, the snowy forest now beginning to drip and plop and squelch in the morning sun, Clarissa berated herself for not being honest with Nordri.

Here this woman bares her soul to you, gives you coffee bread, good coffee bread, delicious coffee bread....

'Marvellous coffee bread.'

Oh, gawd....

She talks honestly, from her gut, about her life, her fears, her needs before she dies, and what do you do? Lie. Is that what you did? Lie? Socially polite and acceptable lying.

Nor would you listen to her.

Forget it. Just go back and work.

Work is not why you're here.

Forget why you're here.

As she walked, she noticed her dog limping slightly.

"Damn. Is this exercise too much for you?"

She knew the dog had the genetic disorder of hip dysplasia, a malformation happening to many purebred dogs, probably from in-breeding, and especially in German shepherds who were bred with low, angulated hips and heavy bones.

"I'll give you a pill at the cottage."

Taking her briefcase out of the car, she realized she would have to get the generator going. Electricity was needed for a good reading light and for recharging her computer batteries. No running water, though. The pipe to the Lake had never been put in, the pump never hooked up, not since.... Sponge bathing would have to do.

After pushing a pill down Tasha's throat, Clarissa routed through the bookcase to find the instruction manual.

Gull Rock Operating Manual. Sure Mother prepared it. I can tell. It's so organized, so neat. So complete.

She did it for us, for Andrew and his family, and for me.

"Come on, Tasha."

Taking the heavy car battery out of the trunk of her car, she and Tasha went out to the small cabin hidden in the woods to connect up the generator. The Jennyhaus, it was called. Although her father had showed her once how to connect the battery and start the generator, she still found it necessary to refer to the manual.

Now I've got electricity if I need to work. Don't thank Mother, of course. Never thank Mother.

You're not here to work, Clarissa.

To hell with why you're here. Work. Set your computer up by the window in the living room.

Hours later, past lunch, past supper, for exercise, and for a break, she trudged the cratered beach of pebble-strewn sand owned by a neighbour.

'Nobody owns the land. They only steward it.'

Or ruin it.

As she walked, the Lake was a translucent veil, crumpled by occasional swells that arced in varying cadences into the irregularities of the beach to create the echoes and variations of a fugue, sound chasing and echoing itself.

Wavelet. Cresting. Absorbing into the sand. Backwash of tinkling agates. Sunset lights of amethyst and green, fuchsia, and blue.

"Hey, here are those big footprints again. Yes. Huge. Bigger than yours, Tasha."

Wolf. Not big enough for a bear. Only four toes showing, not five like a bear.

More than one set of tracks. Maybe a pair. Maybe more. They won't hurt me, but I'd better not let Tasha out alone at night.

Wavelet. Cresting. Absorbing into the sand. Backwash of tinkling agates. Sunset lights of amethyst and green, fuschia, and blue.

"Oh, look at this agate."

Is it really an agate? Or did Mother call everything an agate?

"Wait, Tasha."

These stones are so beautiful, so smooth. Some striped like a zebra. Here's one that's amber, a Henry Moore shape....

Mother said that.... Or did she say it about the icebergs? What was it Andrew told me? I forget. I wonder how her journal's selling. Andrew found a publisher. He thought it was that good. A portrait, he said.

A portrait of what?

Unkind.

I suppose I should read it.

Yeah, right.

What did Andrew call it? The Survivor of the Edmund Fitzgerald? Strange title. Officially there were no survivors.

Whose story is it supposed to be anyway? It was her journal.

Does Lake Superior really have icebergs?

"Shut up.

"Not you, Tasha. My mind.

"Oh, let's just sit here on these soft stones for a while...."

'Soft stones!'

How can this place ever be mine? She's everywhere. Her handiwork. Her loves. Her death. Andrew and I found her body about a half mile from here, to the south, somewhere between here and Nordri's place. In her turret, which we never took the trouble to see. Of course, it overlooked her beloved Lake.

High up on one of the rock outcrops, nestled under an aiguille, a little sheltered, palisaded lookout.... How did she ever get there? That guy, the supposed survivor of the Big Fitz, that stowaway who jumped ship just as it was sinking, he must have helped her. Dad said he didn't exist, just a figment of Mother's mind, frantic with illness and pain.

Yet his voice was on the tape recorder.

Or was it hers, acting out the male? Carl Jung said each gender incorporates its opposite. In her delirium, maybe....

Andrew figures the survivor existed, but where he went, who knows?

Jokingly Andrew said maybe that guy was a trapped soul, unable to die and be at peace because he believed he was a coward for not warning the crew. Just wandering the frozen shore. Until he encountered Mother.

Jokingly?

I really should read her journal!

Mother struggled so hard to get away from here, from GULL ROCK, from the place that she loved, to die somewhere else so we wouldn't be haunted by her body being found here.

It's not her death that haunts me. It's her life.

You're haunted by your life, you mean.

You wouldn't give her the time of day. What was the matter with you? She was the only mother you'll ever have and you had no truck with her.

Look at you. You're a decent person, good values, hard worker, honest, fine upstanding citizen, not a druggie or a boozer or a sexie. You've got guts. How'd you get that way, eh?

She devoted her life to you. Gave up her profession. Put her family first. Always put her family first. What was it she'd say? 'The children are the future.'

Now you've got to decide if you want this place. Dad is having lots of trouble coming back here. Can't come here alone, he says. Wants it to be a family place, and if no one will come, then he wants it to be a family decision to sell it. Either we all come here, or we let it go. He knows Mother wanted this place as a legacy to us and the children to come, there's so little wild land left, but we all feel such guilt, such remorse, at her having to die alone, having to muster such strength all on her own because she wanted death on her own terms, but without legally implicating anybody.

Andrew doesn't know what to do, either. Up to me, he said.

Why did I run when I saw she looked old and sick? Why didn't I just take her in my arms and thank her for being such a good mother?

I got on the plane as soon as I could and went back to Toronto. Next thing, Dad calls me and says she has gone to the cottage. In winter. By herself. Although I was reluctant, Andrew and I skied in, but it was too late.

'Rational suicide.' That's what she called it.

Guts? Did she have guts, or didn't she? Rhetorical question. No siren song of 'help me' then.

But you, Clarissa, you've got no guts. You ran when she was ill because you saw death, worse, you saw aging and dying, so you ran. You were mad at her for reminding you of this. Now she's so strong in your life, she's overpowering you, not that she really intended that, but this place, it's living and breathing HER. Where am I, the thing that is the I of Clarissa? How can I come here? I can't be me.

"Come on, Tasha. Better get back."

The sun's gone down and it'll be dark soon. Shouldn't have stayed out so long. It's cooling off. I've gotta get the fire stoked up. There's no wind, not even a ripple. Well maybe, there's always a ripple on Lake Superior.

"Come on, girl. Let's go."

The disappearing light in the west was pulling darkness over the earth. Clarissa was on the verge of panic by the time she got back to the house and almost ran as she brought the big blocks of maple firewood into the cabin. She was glad of the floodlights provided by the generator, although the hum of its noise, albeit muffled, always bothered her.

'Better than the swath of a hydro line.'

Mother's thought, of course.

"Come on, Tasha."

She jogged to the Jennyhaus and locked it, as she always did, and jogged to the loo, as she always did; then she checked the locks on the shutters on the low windows. Inside, she snapped closed the deadbolts on the two doors.

What am I doing here, anyway?

Leave tomorrow.

§§§

Sometime during the blackness of night, the intruder alarm sounded, Tasha first barking in a desultory way, which Clarissa ignored in her sleep, then, the dog barking more frantically, loudly, its pitch rising. Clarissa realized it was the dog's serious bark, and she woke up.

Clarissa switched on her flashlight and ran downstairs. She grabbed the gun from the rack and three shells from the cosmetic case in the drawer. Resting the flashlight on the dresser, she snapped the chamber of the gun closed and inserted two shells underneath into the magazine tube.

Can I see by this rotten light? Don't want the generator on yet.

Slowly. Don't jam it.

She pulled back the stiff lever to open the chamber and inserted another shell.

Now snap it closed, but don't take the last safety off.

Yet.

She filled her pyjama pockets with shells and hid the cosmetic case at the back of the drawer. Be prepared for anything, she thought. She switched off the flashlight. Carrying the gun, she padded in her bare feet to the high window by the door and flipped on the floodlights, the generator beginning its low hum. Figures dove for the shadows. Clarissa felt her hair prickle and a tight feeling develop in the back of her neck. Fear. Out-and-out fear. She had never experienced it before.

She carefully felt her way upstairs to the bedroom and searched for her clothes in the shadows of the floodlights. She pulled on jeans and a plaid shirt over her pyjamas, transferring the shells to a shirt pocket, the pockets in her jeans too tight for anything. She put on shoes and socks.

The floodlights went out. The windows went dark. The hum stopped.

They've cut a wire.

"Stoo-pid. I shouldn't have put on the lights," she whispered to the dog, standing by the door, now growling a low, guttural growl, its legs stiff, its ruff up.

"Lady, we're coming in."

"You ain't got no chance."

Clarissa crept to the window, her eyes adjusting to the blackness. How many were there? Three? Four? One well-spoken. The others rough? Did it matter?

"Lady, we know you're alone."

How'd they know that?

Thankgawd I left those low windows shuttered.

"Yur dog means nothin' to us. We've got a baseball bat. And a couple a axes. We're gonna hack our way in."

Maybe axes and baseball bats should be registered. Like guns.

She snapped off the screen and opened the window. She took the last safety off the gun and fired in the air. The spent cartridge flew out and the recoil knocked her back, but she held tightly to the gun. She knew about its kick.

She saw figures dive for the trees. Two of them had bottles in their hands.

"Your gun means nothing."

"Nothin'."

"There's four of us and we're coming in."

"Ya can't get all of us."

"Spread out, guys."

They're drunk.

She heard a window shatter. But she knew it would take them a while to make the big thermopane window safe enough to climb through, if they could get up to it. All the ladders were locked away.

Then she heard an axe chop at the front door. Then at the back door.

The dog was now frantically running around downstairs, barking, growling.

"Come here, Tasha."

The dog obeyed.

Mother insisted on training.

In the shadows, Tasha looked like a porcupine the size of a small bear, her fur so bristled and standing on end. Like Clarissa's hair.

She closed the upstairs bedroom door and wedged a chair under the handle. She ran out on the deck, followed by the dog.

Clarissa fired the gun again. Into the air.

One shell left. Better reload. Can I do it in the dark?

The moon, gibbous and hunching towards her, emerged from the shadows.

"Thanks, moon."

Safety on.

Two shells in underneath. One already in the chamber.

Safety off.

I don't want to shoot anybody.

But I will if I have to.

Think of the alternative.

They're so drunk they don't realize I could get take them all out one by one. But I don't want to.

You'd have to reload, remember.

"Now get this, you guys. I'm calling for help. And, I'm going to get it. You better get out of here."

"Yeah. Yeah. Lady."

"We know you don't have a phone."

"We checked yur car. You ain't got no cell-u-lar. No towers. We know."

Clarissa knelt down on one knee. She put down the gun.

"Okay, Tasha."

I'll take that wish now, Mishipishu.

She grabbed the dog tightly by the collar, the way she had done when she had cajoled her to howl. Clarissa raised her head to the hunched, gibbous moon and, saying a silent prayer to her inner strength, let out a rising, wailing wolf howl.

Answer me. Answer me.

"She's gone nuts."

"Lady. You're crazy."

After several howls, the dog, squirming, resisting, not wanting to, raised its head and crooned a low, mellifluous howl from its big, well-bred chest.

"You'll see. I can call the wolves. So can my dog. They're our friends. They'll get you."

"Yeah. Yeah."

Clarissa and the dog howled and howled again.

Silence. No sound. The Lake still. Wavelets. Cresting. Absorbing into the sand. Backwash of tinkling agates.

Then, howls. Howls sang out, coming from down the beach.

"Didja hear that?"

"It was an echo."

"It was not."

Thank you. Thank you.

Clarissa howled again and her dog howled.

Silence.

Howls again from the shore. This time closer. Much closer. Now coming from the crevasse between the serac-like rocks on the shore. Almost in front of the house.

"They're comin'."

"She's a witch."

"A witch."

"I'm outta here."

"Jesus. Where's the flashlight? We gotta go down that road."

"Let's go before they get closer."

"They're gonna come after us."

"You're right," Clarissa called. "They'll get you, if I tell them to. So get outta here. And never come back."

"Come on."

She and the dog howled again.

The wolves answered.

"Thank you," Clarissa called.

Clarissa cried and laughed and hugged the dog.

She and the dog sat on the veranda for a long time even though it was cold. They watched the moon arc down the sky. For a while, they saw the shadowy forms of the wolves on the beach, lean and spectre-like compared to the shepherd. No hip dysplasia there.

She lit the back-up propane lights, had a snack, put wood on the fire, turned off the lights, and went to bed. Her eyes would not stay shut.

Too much adrenalin. What to do?

The journal. Mother's journal. I'm sure I packed it. Might as well read it. What's it called? The Survivor of the Edmund Fitzgerald?

"I hope Nordri's all right. She will be. Those guys'll head straight for the gate and their car."

The Journal

The Survivor of the Edmund Fitzgerald
A journal by Clara Wheatley

ANDREW WHEATLEY, editor

IN THE NORTHERN COLD of early February, my sister Clarissa, with some persuasion, and I went to see our mother, Clara Wheatley. Our father told us she was ill and had gone to the family cottage on the north shore of Lake Superior, west of Sault Ste. Marie.

We first found Mother's journal, partly typewritten, partly taped. Shortly afterwards, we found her body.

After reading her journal, I can only think of what Moses said: "Then shall the man be guiltless, but the woman shall bear her iniquity."

Apart from the sorrow, the admiration, and the guilt it brought to our family, the journal gives a fascinating perspective to the mysterious sinking of the *Edmund Fitzgerald* in Lake Superior on November 10, 1975.

Officially, the *Fitzgerald* — "the *Titanic* of the Great Lakes," as Mother called it — sank with all hands. In her journal, slightly edited by me, she tells otherwise. As well as her own story, she recounts the hitherto unknown story of the only survivor of the *Edmund Fitzgerald*.

Each lends a special meaning to the word "survive."

ANDREW WHEATLEY, MD

JANUARY 20, 1976 · I want to explain. And oddly enough I want to tell you about something interesting, a bit of intrigue here in the wilderness of Lake Superior, a bit of mystery in which I find myself involved.

As you now realize, I am at the cottage. At GULL ROCK.

I encountered the strangest person. He was weird.

With difficulty, I had made my way to our favourite ridge overlooking the Lake. Grandly, we call it Bald Mountain. I had always wanted to see it in winter, but your father pooh-poohed my suggestions, kindly, of course. I never insisted, nor would I go alone.

None of those excuses for me now. I wanted to see it, and I did.

Of course, I had trouble getting up the steep ledge, and not just because of my weight. Yes, despite my illness and losing weight, I am still, shall we say, pleasingly plump.

Pulling on the branches of a helpful red pine, apologizing when I broke some branches, I grabbed a clump of needles and almost nimbly pulled myself to the top.

If I had tried to climb up there last year, I would have had to grab the trunk!

Stop joking.

Perspiring and out of breath, and in pain, I pawed at the top of a billowing snowdrift to locate the boulder that I knew was there.

When I sat down I wondered where those huge rocks came from. Hudson Bay? Russia? Quebec? Deposited here not so long ago in geological time by the immense Wisconsin Glacier, what was I, my silly jokes, my short life, my suffering, in a time frame like that?

Well, the suffering is something to me, all right.

I just sat and absorbed the view. Lake Superior in winter. A goblet of blue in fingers of white.

Marvellous view.

It is January, and parts of the Lake are still not frozen. Of course, Lake Superior hardly ever freezes completely. Those translucent patches of open water remain like panes of blue glass looking out curtains of white....

Forgive me for lavishing these words on the Lake.

I was just about to think those blue openings of water were like windows to another world, when the forest at the far end of the ridge began to move.

Something coming out of the forest?

I stood up.

What?

No, who? Almost like a person from another world. More like a walking snowman. A man. Canting from side to side as he plunged one foot, then the other, down into the deep snow. In places, snow was drifted to maybe three feet. Icicles were hanging from his hat and his beard. As he lumbered towards me I could see his eyes were icicled with white lashes.

He must be almost frozen to death.

I hope.

Don't say that.

But what would any normal human being be doing roaming around out here?

The question applies to me, I thought. To me, Clara Wheatley.

Expecting to see a death mask for a face, I was surprised to see he was vibrant and youthful with clear blue eyes, and not looking the least bit cold.

However, those clear blue eyes had a startled, panicked, look to them, a look I have only seen once before, and that was in your eyes, Andrew, after you almost died in the auto accident. The look did not go away until you came to terms with what happened to you.

"Hi there," he said.

"Ah.... Hi," I replied.

Maybe he was one of those handsome crazies who charm their

victims first? Of course, I did not have the dog with me. I left her at home with Jeff. And the gun was in the cabin.

He looked so young, so healthy, more like a bearded Peter Pan than....

"Did I scare you?" he asked.

"I thought you were ... ah ... I thought you might be ... ah ... I thought you were a ghost. Yes, a ghost, someone who would be ... frozen to death out here in the cold."

"Don't worry," he said.

You would think I was the most attractive woman in the world. Oh, I am not bad, I guess. For fifty. My figure is a little better now that I have lost some weight. But my hair....

"Lady, I like your dark roots."

But no matter what state of attractiveness, no matter what age, a woman never gets over the horror of molestation, of rape, a legally outdated term, I realize, but not an outdated experience. A woman never gets over the horror of bodily invasion. Men just do not have that basic, almost primeval fear. I even used to be worried about skinny-dipping. Some minnow or eel might....

And there are such a lot of crazies around now, crazies with nice appearances, nice manners, but with a strange, hidden twist that must be satisfied, satisfied by some sort of weird behaviour, some violent power trip, usually involving women and children and sex and death.

Of course, with me, it would be the crazy who was taking the chance.

"Aren't you exhausted?" I asked him. He must have walked at least two or three miles, maybe farther, depending on where he was staying.

"No, I am all right," he said.

He seemed all right.

Through the shroud of snow that enveloped him, I could see that he was young, maybe twenty-five, with a sensitive, rather babyish face in spite of the rubble of beard that looked like it had been trying to grow for some time.

"You live around here?" he asked.

Despite my new-found bravado, I answered carefully, without saying exactly where. Of course, all he had to do was follow my footprints.

He asked about the weather, about the red pine that dominated the ridge, about the depths of snow in winter. He asked about the markings in the snow.

"Oh, those tracks like a baby's hands are raccoons', although there aren't supposed to be any raccoons around here.

"Those little snowshoe prints are actually rabbits'.

"Those ones? Like a string of crochet stitches? Oh, you don't crochet?"

"You like to joke, don't you?" he said.

Then he asked me about the tracks that looked like a dog's but were in single file.

"Oh, those were made by a fox," I said. "Maybe a wolf."

On and on until I realized he was carefully controlling the conversation. Although the verbal ball appeared to be swinging back and forth, it was carefully being manipulated by this young apparition standing in the snow in front of me.

So? What was new? I had always been pliable, passive, talking, joking about whatever anyone wanted, a backboard for anyone to hit the verbal ball against. I decided it was time to move from being a backboard to being a player.

"I seem to be answering a lot of questions," I said. "Why don't you tell me what you are doing walking around here in the snow, miles from civilization?"

"Is it usually this cold here in January?"

"This isn't cold," I said. "But come on, did you come from the highway? From Coppermine Point?"

Without a word, he turned around and slowly lumbered back

across the clearing, canting from side to side as he stepped into one deep footprint after the next. He seemed to vanish into the snow even before he came to the edge of the woods.

My first venture into assertiveness had not turned out very well.

JANUARY 21 · This is the high point of my day, this journal to you, my children. Well, you are hardly children at the ages of twenty-two and twenty-four; Andrew, you, a remnant of slavery, a medical student, and Clarissa, you, funnelling your sensitive brain into chartered accountancy.

I can no longer sit to type. I have my typewriter on the buffet and I am standing to type. It works surprisingly well.

My skills as a typist have not deserted me.

In fact, I am thoroughly enjoying being able to write my own words for once. All I ever did when I was a legal secretary was express other people's thoughts.

"Take a letter, Mrs. Wheatley."

"Draw up these documents for me, Mrs. Wheatley."

"Send this information to Jackson, at Jackson, McMillan."

Often I knew the law better than the lawyers did.

It is January cold. The cabin is warm and snug even though the temperature is fifteen below. Fahrenheit, that is. On the Celsius scale, that would be, what? Twenty-five below? Why this tampering with our national scale of measurement? No doubt a bureaucratic power play. Next, they will be declaring Ontario bilingual. Or lighthouses will be manned by what is even more fallible than human beings: computers.

Or our dollar bills will be changed into coins!

Quit joking, Clara. You are here to be serious.

Yesterday, as I began this journal, I said that I wanted to explain to you, my adult children, the reasons behind my actions. I want you to understand. It is important to me that you understand.

Yet I find myself more willing to talk to you about other things....

That guy was here again.

I looked out and there he was rambling around in his shroud of snow and ice, looking like it was he who was ready to lie down in the snow. He began poking around my car, even though it was almost impossible to tell it was there, it was so buried.

Then he seemed to disappear.

Where did Jeff put that gun?

Forget it. In my damned dependency, in my earlier damned dependency, I never even learned how to use it. So I grabbed my ski jacket and went outside. Better than him getting in. No fear of rape out there. That cold was going to stop the exposure of anything. It was too cold!

"Hi there," he said. "Did I startle you again?"

"No, not this time," I answered.

His eyes still had that look, the look that is so difficult to describe.

"I was just going to get you some wood."

"Oh, I've got lots of wood inside. Don't bother."

Liar, liar, the truth's for hire....

He was not going to use *that* ruse to get inside.

We went through the usual chitty-chat about the weather. There we were, two individuals in the starkest of winter cold. I, clutching an unzipped ski jacket across my chest, he, caked in ice, talking about the weather as if we had met in the canyons of Bay Street in Toronto. As the wind swirled around my car, it nothing but a hillock in the snow, it tore at his scarf, his parka. For the first time, I noticed that his legs were encased in black pants, shiny black pants, almost like a wetsuit.

"I'm Gene Amort," he said.

"Gene. Not a girl's name. G-e-n-e. As in...."

"I know."

"I'm an artist from Toronto."

That figures, I thought.

"I'm Clara Wheatley."

"Are you sick? You look very pale," he said.

I lied again and said I was all right. My teeth were beginning to chatter. Do you know what I did? I asked him if he would like to come inside and have a cup of tea. He looked cold, too.

"Come on in," I said. "You look half-frozen to death."

As we walked towards the door, I heard him repeat what I had said, "Half-frozen? Half-alive?"

While I waited for the water to boil, we chatted. I asked him where he was staying.

"Across the bay at a cottage, or camp, to use the northern Ontario terminology," he said.

A touché slam against northerners, calling their summer places camps. We're all Boy Scouts up here, you know.

"Near Coppermine?"

"Actually, yes."

"That's a long walk from here. It must be very tiring because of the snow drifts and the rubble ice around the shore, and it certainly would be risky walking across the Lake."

He told me that he had indeed walked across the Lake over the ice.

"Don't you realize that's the open water of Lake Superior out there?" I asked. "That it's always pushing on the ice, cracking it, buckling it?"

"So?"

"I wouldn't want to look out and see a hand sticking out of a crack, knowing it's you heading feet first towards Davey Jones's locker."

"No. It would be head first."

"Pardon?"

"Sorry. Just a little personal joke."

"Well, just remember my advice," I said. As you know, a mother can never stop giving advice.

"In all the years that we've owned this place, only once have we ever skied out to Gull Rock," I said.

"You mean that mound of ice out there is a rock?"

"A rock island that's a gull rookery in the spring and summer. But there's no life there now."

"No death there, either," he said.

"Pardon?" I said.

"When I saw the smoke from your chimney, I followed it like a beacon. I thought I would see who else might be trying to live on this desolate stretch of Lake Superior at this time of year."

I corrected him. "It's not desolate. You only *perceive* it to be desolate. It's only desolate to you. A lot of the life around here is just sleeping, the bears, the insects, the leaves.... Besides, there are the foxes, and the rabbits. Maybe raccoons. Maybe wolves. You saw their prints in the snow. And the mice.... Oh, the poor mice. Which cottage do you own?" I changed the subject from the mice because it made me feel so guilty.

"I don't own a cottage."

"You are renting? Renting at this time of year? Or maybe visiting?"

"No."

"No to what? Renting or visiting?"

"No to both."

"I don't understand."

"I am not visiting. I am not renting."

What on earth is he trying to say? I asked myself.

"I broke into somebody's place."

"You what?"

"I had to stay somewhere. I'm not making a mess or anything. I'll leave a little money when I go. I just need a place, a halfway house, for a while until ... until I get some things sorted out."

I didn't know what to say. A B&E in my living room!

"I'm not going to hurt anything. Or anyone."

"I'm glad to hear that."

"Did I scare you?"

"Well…. Are you in trouble?"

"I don't know."

"That's not much help."

"Maybe I just need someone to…."

"Aren't you afraid I will tell someone? Call the police?"

"Somehow I don't think you will," he said, looking around at the wilderness log cabin with its propane lights and lack of telephone, knowing, of course, my car was buried in the snow, the road impassable.

"I'll go and make us some tea. The best solution to anything."

When I came back with the tea, he'd gone.

In an irrational moment I had invited a stranger into my living room. How did I know he was not one of those charming crazies? And then he just disappears.

I do not really think he is a crazy. But then what is he?

Why is he coming around here?

JANUARY 22 · I can no longer stand to type. Neither sitting nor standing is comfortable for any period of time. I have decided to finish this journal on my little tape recorder so that I can move around while I am talking to you. Bear with me. I am not used to doing this.

Pain is such a mind-expanding experience. Or maybe a mind-shrinking experience. However, it is kind of interesting, in an academic sort of way, to learn the limits of endurance. My endurance. Interesting, but I cannot say particularly desirable, although I have found out I am a lot tougher than I, or anyone, would have thought.

For you, Andrew, studying medicine, it is so important that you have known pain first hand. Frankly, I think anyone to qualify as an MD should be required to have a broken bone and to spend at least one week flat on their back in a hospital bed. Then they would find out what it is like to depend on others for their comforts. They would find out just what the smallest gesture of kindness can mean. What it is like to eat hospital food....

You see, there are no words to describe pain. Words are symbols for something, symbols that we agree on to describe an experience that seems to be mutual. But pain is no mutual experience. It is mine. I can tell you what it does to me, but I cannot tell you what it is.

What pain did to me last night was to give me a bad night's sleep; well, a sleep worse than usual, I should say, despite the painkillers. Consequently, I slept in late and the fire in the Jøtul was virtually out by the time I got up. As I took some kindling and newspaper to restart it, my teeth chattering, having to go to the loo, I found this story in the newspaper on the sinking of the *Edmund Fitzgerald*. I could not help glancing through it, and I put it aside to read more thoroughly later. No, I am not running out of reading material, but the kind of reading I can do under the influence of painkillers is, well, limited.

Remember the night of the sinking? November tenth, 1975? The Sault took the brunt of it. Little did we realize that date would go down in history. Little did I realize I was ignoring a storm that would go down in history. Gusts up to ninety-five miles an hour. I remember the broken-off spiny tips of our tamarack trees hitting the window; the dull, vibrating thud through the floor when they blew over, the wind obscuring the sound of the fall, but not the sensation; I remember when I opened the door to get the newspaper the storm sounded like a freight train roaring over the roof. The sinking was the greatest financial loss on the Great Lakes ever. And so mysterious.

Clarissa, you were furious with me because I suggested you not go out. You were, maybe still are, at that stage of rejecting Mother, no matter what I do or say.

Oddly enough, I remember the night more because of what happened to your father than for what happened on the big Lake. It was not until the next day that we realized what really was the *Titanic* of the Great Lakes, the *Edmund Fitzgerald*, sank right out in front, well, to the northwest, about twelve miles out. Right out there. Twenty-nine men were lost.

Do you suppose bodies might wash up here? Gordon Lightfoot's song, "The Sinking of the Edmund Fitzgerald," says Superior never gives up its dead. That is not always true. For instance, bodies washed up for days after the sinking of the barge, the *Olive Jeanette*, and its towing ship, the *Iosco*. The captain was found lashed to the mast. Usually, though, in Lake Superior the water is so cold the bacteria that causes a body to rise to the surface just cannot grow. I have read of a ship's cook that was found floating in his sunken galley some twenty years after the sinking. I read of a diver that encountered a cow suspended near the bottom of the Lake as if it was alive. Ugh!

Anyway, I remember November tenth because I was worried about your father, who was later than usual for dinner. As you know, lawyers are always late for dinner. He worked such long hours, never billing for all his time; if he was paid a plumber's hourly rate we would have been millionaires! Anyway, your father stayed at the courthouse to help a judge threatened by a disgruntled parent who just lost a custody battle. Although courthouses are fortresses in London, Toronto, and Ottawa, the security in smaller cities is a laugh. The constable guarding the judge, a dear little old lady, said when she heard about the parent going to shoot "de effen judge," she said to the judge: "I don't know about you, Your Honour, but I'm going home." So much for the security!

By the way, the word was not "effen," but she would not say that other word. Nor would I, as you know.

You probably do, Clarissa.

Jeff waited for the judge to sign the custody order, and then he escorted him to the car.

All this in the middle of that howling mêlée of a storm.

While we laughed and joked about the government's assumption of the invulnerability, or dispensability, of judges—northern Ontario judges, that is—a supposedly invulnerable ship was literally gulped down by Lake Superior. There had not been a major sinking in twenty-two years and I guess everyone figured they had beaten the Lake.

No one can ever beat that Lake. Nothing is invulnerable. It is false pride—no, *dangerous* pride—to think so.

It was right out in front, you know. Twelve miles out. Of course, I have repeated that fact many times. I apologize. Repetition begins at fifty. You will see. Unfortunately.

The *Fitzgerald* sank off Coppermine Point in Canadian waters. However, everyone is saying, even Canadian media, that it sank in Whitefish Bay off Whitefish Point. On the American side of Lake Superior! We are even losing our shipwrecks to the Americans?

If we had been here, which we were not, and if the visibility had been good, which it was not, it was squalling snow, we would have seen those lights disappear from the horizon.

It must have given the captain of the *Anderson*, the ship following the *Fitzgerald*, an eerie feeling to see it happen. No Mayday call. No distress message of any kind. "We're holding our own," were the captain's last recorded words. Then it sank.

Oh, I know how I am avoiding talking to you, avoiding saying what is most important to me.

My Clarissa, my Andrew, you both have turned out to be honest, hard-working, independent individuals. You will pull your weight in society. If you ever get out of school, that is. I mean you, Andrew. Pardon my wisecracks. You know me.

Seriously though, if the world was comprised of individuals like you, there would be no trouble. I am very proud of you. It is high time I said it.

I am so pleased my half-completed education did someone some good. You have benefited. Even though I quit law school after the first year in order to get married and work as a legal secretary to help your father become the lawyer in the family, I have never regretted what I did. I was able to give a background and richness to three people's lives. Does it sound smug and egotistical to say so?

Am I here to try to justify myself, to justify my life, my existence?

I have not particularly liked feeling like a second-class citizen, or losing all I had gained with my academic prowess. I have not liked being unable to get a credit card without my husband's name, or women looking towards the first man that walks into a room, or having tradespeople asking to deal with "the man of the house," or stewardesses on planes and waitresses at fast-food counters waiting on men first.

It all seemed a continuation of that paradise-lost existence into which I was plunged after my brother's birth....

Now, just now, I realize I have not liked having to use all those dyes, for my eyes, my lips, the goop to make my hair blond. Can we trust the government to say it's safe? And those high heels! How they hurt my back and feet. I spent so much time shopping for clothes. Why did I do it? To feel some pride in myself? To please men? To overcome the feeling that on the male stage, on the neuter stage, I was a bit player? So at least *look* sexy? It certainly gave some power.

My one big play, the staging of an anti-pollution rally, had its glory kicked out from under it by a friend. Friend? I had worked feverishly on preparations and publicity for the rally, mainly because of you, my children. I could visualize only too well the long-term effects of foreign substances dumped into the living room of our environment. It was an idea almost ahead of its time, but we managed to muster some community and political concern. It gave me a role of leadership; I made speeches; I was listened to. Not since law school had faces turned towards me to hear me speak.

Afterwards, sitting around basking in the glory of success, a little wine loosening the shackles of niceties, my friend said to me: "Clara, you know the only reason you were able to make this rally a success?"

"What?" I asked. Thinking of the nice compliments that might follow.

"Your husband's name made it a success."

"My husband's name?"

"Yes. Because of his position, his name, his influence in the community, you commanded respect. Doors were opened for you."

Oh, the slights and putdowns a woman has to endure. Even from other women!

Clarissa, I don't know if it's better for you, or worse. The slights and putdowns maybe are less, but actual violence against women is erupting instead. What is happening?

I saw a plane fly over today. It was a small plane gliding along the shoreline like a gull searching for food. Could someone have been looking for me? The smoke from the chimney would have been a giveaway. I left many clues to a false trail, even a sealed letter to Jeff to open only if he absolutely needed to get in touch with me. It contained a plea to leave me alone, difficult, I know, for a husband of thirty years.

Our relationship has not been good recently.

That Gene Amort has not been around. It was sort of nice having the company, even though he worried me a little. I miss Tasha. A dog is such good company.

I am pretty sure Gene is not a crazy. He has a funny look in his eyes, though.

I wish you could see the sun shining in prisms through the frozen air. The new snow that fell during the night is like goose down over the land, and there is that smell, that delightful smell of winter in the air. On the way back from the loo, I walked on the beach in front of the cabin, fluffing up the snow with my foot, simply exulting in being alive.

Marvellous.

That word's been a catch phrase for me. Instead of saying what I thought, I said "marvellous." Never realized it.

Each time I walk, I am saying goodbye.

Goodbye to a place?

James Joyce was asked: "Where are you going?"

He replied: "Home, always home."

But for me, I never knew where home was. Although complacent and accepting as a youngster, I felt alien, alien to my family, alien to my birthplace of southern Ontario, alien to those flat lands and all those people, all those crowds. Naturally, I never said anything. But I was restless, always looking. When I came north, I knew I was getting closer to home; the stunted trees with their roots in rock; the swirling black and red lava; the remnants of a forest primeval. I knew I was closer. I was getting warm, as we used to say when we played those childhood games, the names of which I can no longer remember. When we found this place on Lake Superior, when we found GULL ROCK, with its little log cabin snuggled into the trees, I knew I was home.

I don't actually understand why. I grew up in a city, never knew, never had seen anything like the passionate country of Lake Superior. Yet, here is where I feel at home, where I belong.

I only wish I had known what it meant to be thin, to be agile, free of the nonsense of fashion. How I would have immersed myself in the lore of the Lake first hand, not through books.

JANUARY 23 · Solitude has such an interesting effect on me. It seems to drive me into myself. I am not living in the world, I am living in my mind; my surroundings become my mind; the rocks, the snow-laden trees, the turquoise ice are mine, just like my memories, my thoughts are mine. It is almost as if I am in a dream; everything is mental. I like it, but I want to run from it. No yackety-yak, no television, no structure or obligation where I can hide. Not even the dog to talk to. I am driven, yes, driven, to be an active participant in the phantasmagoria of this spirit world. I understand that ants will die if required to live alone — but humans are not ants, or rats or white mice for that matter, a swipe at the psychologists who like to equate human behaviour to that of their animals in the lab. I can understand why the highs of the human race come from solitudinous individuals, from maverick behaviour of individuals standing alone, acting alone, thinking alone. Solitude impels action.

Its prodding has produced some interesting reading. Despite my mission here, I certainly am not lazing around. I have been reading more about Lake Superior, reading about the sinking of the *Fitzgerald*. Why, I do not know. What good is any reading going to do me now?

I cannot get over the number of ships that have sunk in Lake Superior, over five hundred, and the number of ships that simply "went missing," bad grammar, just like the *Fitzgerald* did. During the First World War, three mine sweepers that were built in Port Arthur, now the city of Thunder Bay, set out in a convoy heading east across Lake Superior to the locks at Sault Ste. Marie and eventually to the Atlantic Ocean. Only one made it to the locks. Nothing was ever seen again of the other two. They disappeared somewhere in Lake Superior. How could two ships vanish without even a signal of distress or radio message? Just like the *Fitzgerald* did, that is how. Mysteriously.

I said that.

But let me tell you about my day. Actually, I am feeling pretty good about my stay here. I am managing quite well on my own, thank you very much. Jeff always ridiculed the idea of me staying here by myself. He said I would be scared, that I could not carry the water, that I could not keep the fire going.

How wrong he was. Each time I open the door of that big-bellied stove and see those flames and red coals, I feel proud. Granted the loss of weight has helped me. Why did I ever lug that extra thirty or so pounds around? Your father did not seem to mind me being fa ... ah ... overweight. Pleasingly plump. He loved to play in my soft body — I should not have said that to you — and he never minded when I had to keep buying new clothes because I grew out of my old ones. He said it kept me out of trouble. Nor did he mind paying the bills for the chiropodist to cut my toenails. He almost seemed to like my dependency. It certainly gave him control. Maybe I liked it, too. It also gave me a certain amount of control. For sure, I did not have to put out the garbage or cut the lawn. He never objected to doing "man's work." And, if he didn't have time to do it, he got you to do it, Andrew. "Help your mother, Andrew. It's too hard for her," he would say.

He never helped in the kitchen, though. Never dried a dish. "Woman's work," he said.

I manage to get water out of the Lake every day, being sure to keep the hole covered with plywood, and marked with a long branch stuck in the snow. It would be so easy to lose the hole in a storm.

I am not even afraid. Before, when everyone left, I felt a cold apprehension. What if a bear came around, or a crazy? I always knew where the gun was hidden, but I never learned how to use it. Did I say that? My defence instead was to bake. And then to eat. My eating, my overeating, was secret, alone, and pleasurable. Like other clandestine pleasures.

I should not have said that.

Change the subject.

In the morning, I stay cuddled under the covers until forced up by the demands of nature. That is another story. We will leave that. Change the subject again. I check the fire, as I said, and eat some breakfast, usually juice, cereal, toast, coffee. Food again. Occasionally, I try to drink some powdered milk. Sometimes, I make a feed of pancakes, or French toast; you know how I love them. Your father hated me using that word, "feed"; and rightly so; however, it was an accurate description of the way I liked to eat. I take my vitamins. Irrational, isn't it? But a good habit is just as hard to break as a bad one. Then I check the mousetraps, dust a bit. Usually in the morning I read, maybe walk, sometimes sleep.

My food is lasting well. But, then, you know me. Would I come here without food? I came supplied with my usual gourmet ingredients: fresh spices, wild rice, butter, frozen meats. And, of course, the root cellar is well-stocked: dried beans, flour, cereals, vegetables like carrots and potatoes. I originally stocked it for you some time ago, my children, and have kept rotating the food. I stocked it in case of a global disaster. The root cellar was my way of trying — laughable, I admit — to defend you against what we are doing to ourselves on this planet, putrefying our air, food, and water, and stashing nuclear arms more than the equivalent of one million Hiroshimas.

How could the world end? Let me count the ways.

And I dust. Did I say that? You know how I always hated dust around. At least it's dirt we can get rid of, not like that chemical dirt that we can never see.

Then I check the mousetraps. I did say that. Bear with me. The mice are really cute. They have big ears and big black eyes, caricatures straight out of the old Walt Disney cartoons. I feel so badly — guilty, in fact — about catching them, but mice and humans cannot co-exist in the same house. I must be a predator. A predator for land, a predator for food, a predator wherever I go. Does it help that I recognize this? That I try not to kill or usurp without good reason? Never wantonly? I have done my best to keep the mice out. I have filled all possible mouse holes with steel wool.

I empty the traps and I bait them again.

I get weighed. I really do not like to see my weight going down so quickly. It is going down for the wrong reason.

I sponge bathe, the best I can do without running water.

The first few days I was here, oh, I was a slob. I revelled in being a slob. Everything got dirty. I was a mess. I think I even smelled. But then I looked at myself and decided some of the old ways were okay. I never went back to wearing those high-heeled shoes, though. Can you imagine I used to wear them around here? No wonder I had trouble on the rocks. No wonder I was crabby, my feet hurt so. It is simply too difficult to dye my hair. My "halo of blond," as your father called it, is gone. It doesn't look too bad. Why did I ever suffer the inconvenience and expense of dyeing it? Why did I ever take the risk of all those possible carcinogens? Men don't. No, I am simply not taking the care with my appearance that I used to. Care? My appearance was my hobby. You must admit that even though I was pleasingly plump, shall we say, I was always stylish.

Did I lavish that attention on myself to prove to myself I was worth it? Why was it necessary to take such pride in my appearance?

Remember when your father's partner walked in the room and saw me wearing that dazzling jade green *décolleté* gown and he said: "Clara, why Clara, what a nice ... what a nice pair of ... ah ... dresses."

And don't you remember, Andrew, when you arrived home at noon with a group of boys and I was just coming home from one of those wicked morning coffee parties, a.k.a sherry parties, wearing that *ensemble* I had purchased at Holt Renfrew in Toronto with the big black hat and black-and-white-striped dress? Your friends all whistled and said: "Wow!" Afterwards you said to me: "Mom, why do you have to look nice all the time? Why can't you just be like other moms?"

You would laugh if you saw me now. Over long underwear, I am wearing your father's jeans, belted and rolled up. My designer jeans were so tight I could hardly wear pantyhose under them. I'm exaggerating, of course. Now I am even wearing an old pair of Jeff's boots with several pair of socks in them to make them fit. I never realized walking could be so fluid in flat heels. Of course, the weight I am losing helps, too.

And then I sit down....

My constraint in talking to you is lessening. It is difficult to disrobe the mind. For the first time in my life, I actually have complete freedom to say what I want in adult company, not skating over the seriousness of our life with the half-thoughts of social conversation. Not being the joker and life of the party.

Yet it is difficult, difficult to drop the mask that got me through life.

JANUARY 24 · It is morning, a glorious, diamond morning that only winter can give. Marvell ... I am on the shore of the Lake. I came down here to get water and then stopped to sit down and find agates. My tape recorder is in the breast pocket of my jacket. The Lake is still open in some places, with a rim of moulded ice around the shore. In the nooks and crannies of the bay, a heavy lace, or embroidery, of round platelets of ice is bobbing lazily in the slow-motion swells. The Lake sounds like it is breathing.

"You came here to find agates, you say?" I can just hear you.

"Mother, your spaghetti's boiling over if you're trying to find agates on a frozen beach in January."

You are right. It is an impossible task. I scrape away the snow and expose the colourful pebbles in their transparent mortar of ice. So soft to sit on in summer. Soft stones.

When I pour water on this mortar, the pebbles become more brilliant but the ice will not let go. I am just sitting here in the soft snow looking at them. How long has it taken them to wear smooth? Some are as hard as gemstones. In fact, some are gemstones; well, semi-precious gemstones. For instance, the garnets and the agates and the jasper, maybe the turtleback greenstone. Occasionally I have come across an agate that has recently broken free from its host rock. It is still in its almost-sexual form, like a man's scrotum. Of course, the correct geological term, I believe, is mammalian, meaning like a woman's breast. The male would never demean his private parts by describing a rock in terms of them. Okay to do it with the female. There is sexism even in geology.

What am I doing thinking about sex? My sex drive has been removed as if with a knife. It has been a powerful, motivating drive around which I, like everyone else, has had to arrange my life. But it has not been particularly good to me. Oh, I realize it gave me you, my children, and for that I am grateful; and don't misunderstand, I certainly experienced the pleasures of the flesh.

It was a wonderful exploration. Typical of our generation. Jeff and I knew little about sex when we met.

Sex was a classic unknown. It ranked with God, heaven, and death.

As a youngster, I knew of its existence only by deduction. What happened to Thomas Hardy's Tess in the misty, midnight forest? I read and re-read the passage. She lay down in the forest and next thing I knew she was pregnant! The condoms in my father's dresser drawer were some sort of thumb protectors. And there never was an explanation about why on Sunday afternoons the house was locked and I had to play outside. Rain or shine.

When Jeff and I married, it was a special voyage of discovery, lovely, dark, and private. Not a community experience like it is today.

At one point in my life, I would have called sex a root pleasure. Are you happy, Sigmund Freud?

But the woman pays. Oh, the woman pays. Don't ever think differently. Throughout history, except for maybe the past few years or so, who has born the shame of pregnancy outside wedlock? The Bible, *Tess of the D'Urbervilles*, *Anna Karenina* leap to mind as examples. Who bears the risk of abortion, the indignity, the spread-eagled indignity of abortion? The risk of birth control? Of exposure to minimally tested devices like, say, the IUD? How much did the infections I had with the IUD contribute to my present problems?

Let's not talk about that.

I think I will lie back and make an angel, arcing my arms and legs back and forth in the soft snow. Remember how you used to do it? Believe it or not, I used to make angels, too, when I was young.

Yes, I was young.

I am lying still. I am being absorbed by the sky. There is no pain.

The sky is being bisected by the vapour trail of a jet. Other than this widening path of white, the sky is an endless blue. The gulls are gone. The sky seems empty without their gliding form.

No life there now.

No death, either.

Neither one without the other. Sounds like a song. It has a beat.

In winter, it seems as if the world of life and striving is gone. There is a timeless, eternal feel to the landscape that makes anything alive feel alien. Even my memories of the gull colony cheering on the stiff-legged chicks approaching the water for their first swim—kwi-kwi-kwi—memories of the drumming of the partridge, the hollow of a deer bed, balls of hair that might be from a bear, the throbbing of a freighter on the horizon on a still day, the flashing beacon of light across the water from Whitefish Point, all these memories of life seem alien in this winter-still landscape.

I suspect the gulls sometimes eat their young. I suspect this cannibalism is the result of the young running helter-skelter into each other's nesting area because of a disturbance, say from a hawk, or a person; sometimes people boat too close; or worse, once I saw a guy, a carpenter who was working for us, land on the island and, while flailing a paddle overhead, he captured a baby gull and proudly brought it back to us, a bit of grey down with an enormous beak and skinny neck. Because of my fury, he guiltily took it down to the water's edge and let it go. Those parents came over and convoyed it back to the rock, the whole colony still circling and screaming in pandemonium. The reverse Midas touch of the human.

How peaceful it is. So peaceful some might say it is boring.

How could they? Look at the way the sun is delicately refracted by the frozen air into splinters of a rainbow.

Maybe I will see a sundog, that ball of rainbow colours caused by the sun bouncing along the clouds. Have you ever had the good fortune to see one? Very rare.

I had better sit up. Shouldn't get too comfortable in the snow. Not yet.

The Lake will soon be frozen, too, maybe frozen right out to the horizon. Time will stop. Even now Gull Rock's cuestal shape is held in an armour of ice, the sounds of the fluffy, grey chicks whose high-pitched cheeps sound over the water and the kwi-kwi-kwi of the colony as it cheers on every activity of every gull from mating to the first swim will not be heard. These signs and sounds of summer life are gone. Only the eternal, the unchanging, is left in the magnifying eye of winter. Did I say this?

I am equating changelessness with eternal. I am not sure such an assumption is correct. I will have to think about that one.

Oops. I can hear voices shouting. "Don't be so serious, Chu…." Actually, it was my uncles who used to say to me, "Don't be so serious, Chu…."

I won't tell you what they called me. I finally shed the nickname at university when I left them all behind. And by then I had left my seriousness behind, too, except for my studies. I had learned to be jolly, just as I had learned to be smiling and nice, just as I had learned to be a backboard for conversation. When I put my studies aside for your father, I was left only with the niceness.

Tennis, anyone?

It was a torts professor who changed the course of my life. Sometime during the first term of law school, I was asked by the professor to stay behind after class.

As I waited while the other students filed out, your father came over to me and said that I had nothing to worry about, that my remarks in class were good.

What did the torts professor want? I waited, quaking, reviewing everything that had gone on in class, reviewing the lecture, how I had answered his questions. I wondered if he wanted me to expand on my remarks, which, in fact, I had thought were rather astute. I also wondered if it might be possible he was going to make a pass at me, me being the only woman, not only in the class, but in the whole four years of enrolment at Osgoode Hall.

Do you know what he asked me?

"Miss Stewart, my daughter has been looking for shoes like yours. Would you mind telling me where you bought your shoes?"

Would you mind telling me where you bought your shoes?

Does that question signify the import of my life?

Oh, how your father and I laughed. You see, Jeff waited for me to come out of the professor's office — and our love affair began.

"Clara! For gawdsakes, are you all right? What are you doing lying in the snow? Let me help you up."

"Gene! Nice to see you. But I'm all right. Just enjoying myself here in the snow and the sun. There, thanks for helping me up."

"Here. Let me carry those pails."

"I'll be glad when the whole shoreline freezes over."

"Why? Won't it make it harder to get water?"

"No. I'm already getting it from a hole I chopped in the ice in that little inlet over there. I'll be glad when the Lake freezes because I really wouldn't want to see any bodies from the *Fitzgerald* thrown ashore by the waves."

"You know about the *Fitzgerald?*"

"Doesn't everybody?"

"Probably not in southern Ontario."

"Indeed. How well I know its attitude to northern Ontario. I'm from there, too."

"You are?"

"Born and educated in old T.O. But I'm a northerner now."

"That's a twist."

"Listen, if people knew how good life is up here, there'd be a caravan of traffic up northern Ontario's obsolete TransCanada Highway. We simply mustn't tell them."

"They'd never leave wall-to-wall peoplesville."

"I know. I know only too well that southern Ontario doesn't think anything exists past Muskoka."

"And, if it does know anything, it isn't worth remembering. And, if something is remembered, it isn't any good."

"But don't worry about the bodies. There won't be any."

"How do you know?"

"She went down too fast. They're all inside."

"How could you possibly know that? What are you drawing in the snow with your foot?"

"Just fiddling. Not drawing. I haven't been able to draw … for ages. I have artist's block. But, regarding the bodies, it's simple deduction."

"What do you mean?"

"The Old Man…."

"The who?"

"Jeezus, Jackson's jock, can't we go? These pails are heavy."

"Well, put them down."

"Chr.... All right.

"The Old Man, the Captain, the Master, well, he didn't even have time to send a Mayday. Or he didn't want to. In fact, I heard he said the ship was holding her own. But he knew. He knew. He'd been sailing for forty-four years. What good would a distress signal do in the biggest storm he'd ever seen?"

"You keep calling the ship a 'her.' You a sailor?

"Where are you going?"

There, off he goes again, carrying those water pails as if they were empty. I am not sure my new-found assertiveness is getting me anywhere.

What is he hiding anyway?

He couldn't be from the *Fitzgerald*, could he? No. If he was, why wouldn't he just walk to the highway, hitch a ride, and become an instant hero? If he was, how did he alone manage to escape?

JANUARY 25 · After cleaning up the cabin, I usually take my reading to the couch and lie down. I am on the couch now.

My mind is often too foggy to read. Words drop from my mind; nouns disappear from their syntax as if they were sucked into black holes. Like, what's the word for the blanket on the chesterfield? You know, it has squares and there's crocheting in between the squares? Yes, that's right: afghan. Fortunately, in this diary to you it is not as bad as what seems to be happening in my thoughts, or what had been happening in my conversations before I left. So many words sucked into those black holes.... Embarrassing....

Mid-morning I take a painkiller, wait for it to take effect, and then make my way to the loo. Medical science should see me. It would hang its collective head in shame. If I had a headache, arthritis, eczema, a broken leg, the medical world would be right there ready to help. Yet faced with this, it simply did not know what to do. Its deity stance was threatened. It did not know what was wrong with me. Consequently, I have been ignored or avoided. Because my intermittent problems did not fit into any known cluster of symptoms that make up what is called a syndrome, I supposedly had no problem. Or I was a neurotic woman. Because my pain was not demonstrated to them by my screaming or crying or flying apart before their very eyes, they did not acknowledge that I had pain. Couldn't they deduce it? I guess not. I already said that earlier, didn't I? Or did I? As the pain got worse, I retreated into myself, afraid I would fly apart and never put myself together again, afraid that I would create a scene or act silly. Why didn't I? Then maybe they would have listened to me. One doctor made me wait a week for a consultation. Another would not return my phone call when I left the message that the pain medication was not working. When I called back I was told to go to the emergency ward of the hospital. Obviously, he preferred to hide from his impotence. Was it egotism that prevented referral outside the city? Finally, I had the sense to drag myself to a larger centre. My unconscious did it, actually. I dreamed I died. I had just bought a fur coat — predator, again — but I was *so* cold — and I dreamed that I just sank down into the soft, dark fur of that coat and died. When I woke up, I realized I must try to find help. But it was too late. I knew it was too late, I should say. However, I was given good, strong painkillers. Oh, forget all this. What does it matter now?

The dawning of assertiveness has come too late.

I had watched in awe as Liz, your Aunt Elizabeth, my sister, broke the grappling hooks of our family. She was determined to chop out an identity, completely unlike her nurturing one. Although she was doted on and adored, she pushed all those loving, outstretched arms away. Aunts, uncles, grandparents — not Great Gran, she was mine — worried about her, asked about her, gave her treats as I looked on in envy.

"Elizabeth, come and listen to *Pita and the Woof.*"

"I don't want to." She swirled her long, black hair over her shoulder and turned away, tilting up her chin in defiance.

"Come on. Name the instruments for us."

"I don't want to name the instruments. And you can't make me."

Why didn't they ask me? I knew all the instruments.

That damned *Peter and the Wolf.*

Oh, the uncles included me in the rides in their new car. I was given a chance to sit in the rumble seat or to stand on the running board. The car design of today has eliminated all this fun. I was always scared, but I did it. I took every crumb of attention I could get even if I was included just because of Elizabeth. I wanted to stamp my foot and shout: "Look at me. Don't just look at Elizabeth. I am a person, too." But I never did. I just smiled, studied harder, and ate. While I was such a "good little girl," Elizabeth became tough, dynamic, independent, a bra-burner before her time.

Now I'm a high-heel burner before my time.

Did you notice she is always called Elizabeth? Never Lizzie, or Liz, or Beth.

To her fury, I called her Liz. Liz-ard under my breath.

Once an uncle said, "Hey, Liz, wanta learn to jitterbug?"

Looking down her aquiline nose, she coolly said, "If you ever call me Liz again, I will never dance with you. Nor will I ever listen to your stupid records again."

Oh, Clarissa, you are so much like Elizabeth, hacking away at the family bonds until you make us bleed. You don't have to walk on us to find yourself.

But you have her assertiveness, her independence, and I am glad.

As you head towards that independence and a career, I hope you will not miss out on that other part of life so precious to women, having a family, feeling that tie to all life as the future thumps and kicks inside you. I could almost tell you were there the moment you were conceived. Don't miss out on this.

Advice again.

Don't think that as a child I was not given attention. I was. I can still see it all. The oldest child, me, having her world stolen by the intrusion of interlopers, first by her brother, then by her sister, me hanging back in the corner with the hem of my skirt in my mouth while vivacious Elizabeth flirted for the attention of the uncles, while brother Vince stood with a beam of sunshine on him, the male child; I so serious, almost frightened by the goings-on. When Elizabeth left, the uncles turned their attention to me by teasing. Vince was never teased.

"Don't be so serious."

"What's your name, little girl?"

"Come on, give us a smile."

"Look at that frown."

One Sunday afternoon everyone had gathered at Grandmother's: uncles, parents, Great Gran, Elizabeth, Vince. I can even remember the menu, a crock of homemade baked beans, cabbage salad, carrots, and roast pork with applesauce. After the usual banter with Elizabeth, the uncles turned to me:

"What's your name, little girl?"

"Doesn't anyone know this little girl's name?"

No. Nobody seemed to know it.

"Well, little girl, what does your mother call you?"

Do you know what I said, stupid, truthful little girl that I was?

"Chubby. She calls me Chubby."

You should have heard the laughing. Everyone laughed so hard no one noticed that I was crying, no one except Great Gran. She took me aside and comforted me. She was the only one that seemed to notice me, not Elizabeth.

She died.

I didn't know what dying meant.

I swear to God after that I stopped being truthful in conversation, and I stopped being serious. I learned to fend off questions with wisecracks, to parry with life as if it were a joke. Except, of course, with my studies. I directed my seriousness with almost brutal intensity into my studies, taking a twisted delight in beating everyone that called me Chubby. You see, from the time of the incident with my uncles, I became Chubby to everyone, everyone except Great Gran.

At university, I registered under the name of Clara and there finally found respect. Women then were accepted on campus as equals, not like it is today where the influence of all those porno videos has turned women into not just sex objects but....

Yes, I saw a couple of those early videos. A friend of mine stumbled on *Texas Chainsaw Massacre* under her son's bed.

"I'm not affected by what I watch," the kid said. My friend agreed her son could not possibly be influenced.

"If media doesn't affect people, then why does the advertising industry thrive?" I replied.

You must realize, of course, I was never obese, ugh, terrible word. I was just pleasingly plump. At least, that is what I kept telling myself.

I have not seen Gene yet today. He will spring out of somewhere, darting, nimble. His eyes most of the time, darting, nimble, like his body, but still with that look of wide-eyed what? Fear?

He seems so ambivalent in his attitude towards me. He wants to talk to me, but then he runs in another direction as soon as the conversation gets interesting. Sort of like what I'm doing. He reminds me of a hunting dog, quartering back and forth over irrelevant ground in search of game.

I hope that game isn't me. I doubt it.

I expect he would get his just deserts if he came ... too close.

He's probably gone for good. Who knows?

JANUARY 26 · Gene is in the kitchen making tea. He must be doing the dishes as well because of all the clatter. Can you hear it on the tape recorder?

"Want sugar and milk in your tea?"

"Yes, please. Want a shot?"

"Sure."

"Would you mind getting it? It's over there. In the hutch."

The factor of distance plays a part in everything I do. I have to be mentally prepared to move. And, oh, how I have to be motivated.

"Pardon?"

"Nothing."

"I'll go pour the tea now. It should be ready."

Can he tell I am in pain? I have often wondered if people knew. I shopped, played bridge, laughed, walked the dog, just like everyone else. Could people tell? Could you tell? I wonder how many others are walking around with the stigmata of pain searing their brain, yet acting as if it did not exist? If I had complained, if people knew I was suffering, I would not be able to pretend normalcy. I would have to admit my suffering to myself because I could see it in their eyes and their actions, in their stunted, embarrassed treatment of me. Those who really are suffering dare not whine. Not if they want to be, quote and unquote, normal.

"Are you talking to yourself?"

"Not really."

See? He swung in and out of the room like he was on a rope. He gyrates around like a monkey in vest and alpine hat tied to the end of a calliope. Quartering, almost frenetic.

"Clara? Who are you talking to? The mice?"

"I hope you don't mind, but I have a little tape recorder going."

"Jeezus. Picasso's pups! What for?"

"Part of my intention in coming here is to write a journal, a journal I want to leave for my children. However, the typing ... ah

... became too difficult ... ah ... it just didn't work out, so I decided to record it. Do you mind that I've taped some of our conversations?"

"Lady, you're lookin' in my jeans."

"Don't be crude."

"Sorry. Been with men too long."

"Anyway, I'd like to introduce you to my children. Andrew and Clarissa, I'd like to introduce Gene Amort."

"That's Gene. Not the girl's name. G-e-n-e. As in...."

"They know."

"I'm an artist from Toronto."

"Gene, I would like you to meet my children, Andrew and Clarissa."

"Uh.... Hi, there."

"Now...."

"Clara, here's your tea."

"Just brandy, please."

"You said you wanted tea."

"I did? Yes, I did. Thanks, I'll have both."

"Suit yourself."

"Have I told you I think Lake Superior looks like the head of a giant bird?"

"Pardon?"

"Well, just look at the map. Use a bit of Rorschach imagining."

"What?"

"You know, those ink blots that psychologists give you to see what you supposedly think of Mother?"

"Uh...."

"Look at the map. Find the lakehead at Thunder Bay."

"Uh...."

"Oh, yes. You can't find it. I forgot you're from southern Ontario.

"Right up there, to the left, the westerly end. That's right.

"The lakehead at Thunder Bay is, in fact, the forehead, the brow.

"Isle Royale is the eye. That's right.

"And Duluth Harbor is the beak."

"So that's where Duluth is."

"And the throat is the Keweenaw Peninsula."

"The Keweenaw...."

"You know it?"

"A shit scratch."

"Pardon?"

"Sorry. I know it.... I've heard of it."

"For your information, the Keweenaw is one of the most beautiful places in the world."

"It is?"

"Forget it. Well, don't you think Lake Superior looks like a bird?"

"I never really thought about it, not until you mentioned it. Clara, I have to talk to you."

"Clean up your language and I'll talk."

"All right. I won't swear. I'm sorry about the language. I was brought up not to swear in front of women.

"But I mean talk. Serious talk. I need your experience, your advice."

"You make me sound ancient."

"You know what I mean. You are older than I am. A looker, though. But you might be able to give me some advice."

"Oh, I could do that all right. But I won't be staying here long. There's something I have to do."

"If there's anything you have to do, I'll help you. I'll even do it for you."

"I don't think you could do that."

"I don't know what you're referring to, and I don't even care. But if you'll just listen to me, I'll do whatever I can for you. You have to admit I've been helpful to you already."

"Yes. I admit that. Do you know what the French call brandy?"

"No."

"*Eau de vie.*"

"I don't know what that means. My ancestry is English."

"Ah-ha. One of those discriminated against unilingual Canadians."

"Clara, forgawdsake. What does brandy mean?"

"It means water of life."

"That's nice."

"If I believed in God, which I don't. I don't believe or disbelieve; both points of view require faith … there's really no evidence either way.... But if I believed in God, I could hear God saying to Himself, 'What can I give those poor struggling creatures on earth to ease their difficulties?' And, he would say to Himself, if he existed, 'the fermentation process.'"

"What a handout!"

"Yes. And dubious like most handouts."

"Clara! Can I talk to you?"

"I had all these uncles. They always used to kid me, 'Don't be so serious.' They would joke and laugh and kid me, for instance, about the recording, *Peter and the Wolf.* I would try to name all the instruments for them and even when I could, they would tease me and tease me. The worst part was they didn't call it *Peter and the Wolf,* they called it *Pita and the Woof.* At school, when the class was asked to name a piece of music by Prokofiev, I said *Pita and the Woof.* The teacher asked, 'How do you spell that?' And, I started P-i-t-a.... I didn't get any further because of the laughing. Even the teacher was laughing! Could you imagine how wolf, w-o-o-f, would have gone over?

"The uncles would tease, tease, tease, asking me stupid questions, as if they didn't know the answer. 'What is your name, little girl?' As if they didn't know. They kept at me and at me, and finally said, 'Well, what does your mother call you?' I made the mistake of answering, answering truthfully. 'Chubby,' I said.

"Oh, I'm repeating...."

"Not to me."

"After that I stopped being so serious. And honest. Except for my schoolwork. Most of the time I was joking, dressing stylishly, soon prancing around on those high heels, with my hair dyed blond, my opinions, my acceptance of practically anything so tolerant that if I had encountered drugs or pornography, which I didn't, I probably would have accepted them as part of being broad-minded.

"But I was called Chubby. I was Chubby until I went to university, where I changed all that."

"Chubby? You don't look very chubby to me."

"Oh, I wasn't fat. I always used to say I was a thin person trapped in a pleasingly plump body.

"But I *was* chubby. Believe me, I was. I never made it to Pennington's. But almost. You know, I've never admitted that before to anyone, let alone myself."

"Clara, can I talk to you now, be serious?"

"I suppose. Oh, go ahead. I'm here to be serious."

"I figure you've got some kind of a problem—but I do, too."

"I know."

"You do?"

"Yes. You were on the *Fitzgerald*!"

"How in hell?"

"Don't swear."

"All right. Well, you see...."

"Are you alive?"

"Oh, for gawdsakes. You said you'd be serious."

"I am."

"Clara!"

"Will you get to your problem?"

"What's that sound?"

"I don't hear anything."

"What in Jesu? It sounds like a snowmobile, maybe two."

"Where are you going?"

"Now, you've got your chance to turn me in."

There he goes. I've never seen anybody move so quickly. He just seemed to disappear.

I guess I'd better answer the door.

"Hello, ma'am. Just came to check your shore to see if anything's around from the *Fitzgerald*. It sank pretty near right out there, you know."

"Yes. I know. What do you expect might wash up?"

"You never know."

"Don't tell me you are expecting to find bodies?"

"More likely life jackets, stuff like that. But who knows?"

"Mind if we check?"

"Certainly not."

"You've got some trees down, ma'am. And that platform with the steps down to the beach has been washed out."

"Officer, I know that."

"Must a went out in the *Fitzgerald* storm."

"It must be difficult to get water."

"Yes.... It's necessary to take the long way round."

"We'll just run over that path down to the lake three or four times with the snowmobile. Should make the walkin' easier."

"You here alone?"

"Ah ... well.... Yes, officer, I am here alone."

"Anything else we can help you with?"

"No. No. Thank you."

"We'll only trouble you again if we find anything. Otherwise, we'll just leave."

"Could I get you some tea?"

"No, thank you, ma'am."

"Thank you for stopping in."

"No trouble, ma'am."

"Bye."

"Bye."

"Thank you again."

"No trouble, ma'am."

"Bye."

I can hear the sound of their snowmobiles. They are down on the beach now. When they were here I kept trying to think of things to keep them here, to keep them talking. I really don't want to be alone with my thoughts. Or with Gene. Yet, oddly enough, that is also what I want. Before, and to some extent now, I always ran away from my thoughts. But this solitude is driving me into myself. I don't live in the world, I live in my mind, in my surroundings that are in my mind: the log cabin, the colourful afghan, the antique armoire. These are mine just like my memories. I feel like I am living in a spirit world. Maybe that is why people avoid solitude, why they fill themselves with mindless television, mindless games, to escape the spirit world. Jeff would not like me to say that. He likes watching games. He always watches games. But solitude, albeit scary, is a high, a high lonely pinnacle, scaled alone.

There, the sound of the snowmachines has gone.

Did you notice that "went" when the officer said "must a went out in the storm"? I always tried to break you kids of that grammatical error. I never heard it anywhere except northern Ontario.

As you noticed, I did not say anything about Gene. I had my chance. I hope my judgment was right.

He wants me to talk with him for a while. It means lingering around for a little longer. I am a little worried about him saying he runs away from things. Wait until he hears what I might have to ask him to do.

JANUARY 27 · I am sitting here with Gene in the living room of the cabin. We were chatting about his life and I realized you might like to hear about it. He has had a pretty interesting time.

Is this becoming his story or what? I really will get to mine, the reason I am here, the reason I feel a need to explain. Soon. I am like a dog, quartering....

Repetition.

It is the afternoon of January 27. Gene found the screen for the door of the wood stove and the inside has become a grotto of luminescent orange, the maple logs radiating colour, the shimmering outlines magnetizing our eyes almost in worship. We sit and stare and chat and sip, lazy, warm, lovely.... Me, listening to my heart pound from the brandy—a sort of waltz, one, two, three—Gene in a cashmere sweater and silk shirt. With gold cufflinks, no less. Odd, you think? I agree. His long eyelashes curling over his restless blue eyes, a bearded Peter Pan. Where did he get those clothes?

"Never mind where I got the clothes. They're unimportant."

"You're listening to what I'm saying on the tape recorder?"

"How can I help it? Here's more brandy."

"Nothing's unimportant."

"I was a little tight-ass rich kid, if you must know. I left home and was living in a condemned warehouse in downtown Toronto. I told you that, didn't I?"

"Pardon?"

"I told you about living in a condemned warehouse in downtown Toronto?"

"You did? No. Correction. You told me about living in Toronto. Not about the condemned warehouse. Or the other, that tight ... ah ... rich-kid bit. Hah! You're forgetful, too!"

A return of my good old incisiveness. Still a prude, though. No, not a prude. Decent. Why does decency have to be anal? Is tight ass today's equivalent?

"I lined the walls with packing boxes. I bought second-hand furniture. I stole electricity...."

"How would you ever do that?"

"Simple. I tapped into a hydro line. My only expense was the phone. I collected plastic cutlery, old wood. I chased rats. I wandered along Queen Street. And I painted."

"That's right. You told me you were an artist."

"When I would get lonely or depressed, I'd return to my *thinks*...."

"Your what?"

"*Thinks*. You know...."

"No, I don't."

"Well, I felt antagonism towards my father, loved my mother...."

"So? For a male, that's normal, isn't it, Dr. Freud?"

"Clara, for gawdsakes."

"Sorry. Continue."

"My escape in childhood was my imagination. Before I went to sleep, when I sat up in trees—I used to climb trees all the time—I would think about all the courageous things I would do. My adventures always involved me as hero. I called these mental adventures my *thinks*. I had a bunch of stock plots that I used to make up for the shortcomings of my life. I never got tired of them. I always went to bed happy. Me as hero. Dashing across the street and pushing a child from the path of a truck, jumping in the water and rescuing someone from drowning, breaking up a fight on the subway when an Indian was being picked on. All embellished, of course, into long fantasies but always ending with me as hero."

"Me Tonto. You Tarzan."

"You're making it difficult. Anyway, my parents favoured my brothers, they favoured my sisters, they never encouraged my art. They never encouraged anything I did. All they encouraged was making money. I needed the *thinks*."

"What did you want to do?"

"Draw, make model airplanes out of match sticks, mould animals, doodle. According to them, my parents, I was a failure. Even

68 |

when I graduated from art college, I was still a failure because what the hell could anyone do with art college? In my ragged jeans, smoking up, and in my warehouse, I was free of them, and I knew they hated it. I had my art, my *thinks*, and the occasional visit from my parents for amusement. Occasionally a girl. Occasionally a guy. How I rubbed my parents' nose in it. I can still see my mother tippy-toeing over the planks in her alligator spikes, my father surreptitiously brushing the dust from his couturier cashmere coat.

"They simply could not understand that I could be happy without money. Money was their measure of worth. No money coming in, no worth."

"Sort of like a housewife?"

"Yeah. Sort of like a housewife.

"They, my parents, simply could not understand that even though I was standing on one leg, I had my arms outstretched and I was in balance.

"I was into drugs and all that, but my art made me keep my head straight. When I was into grass, even chemicals, I never produced anything good, although sometimes the insights were helpful, if I remembered them, that is.

"I went to all the art shows, not just those at the AGO; sorry, the Art Gallery of Ontario."

"I know what AGO stands for. I probably go there more often than most Torontonians."

"I went to the small experimental galleries. And I learned to draw. Oh I learned to draw. The line is the skeleton. Everything hangs on it. I drew and I drew and then when I was ready, I hung paint on those skeleton lines.

"Do you know an artist never says goodbye?"

"I don't know what you mean."

"Things stay in my mind. Like a double exposure in photography. I'm in them and I'm also in me. I carry this weight of two experiences around with me until I start to get it down; then for a while, just for a while, I'm like a triple exposure, I'm three; them, me, the image, heavy, pregnant, weighted down, and then the art sucks the thing, the image, the person, the design, out of my mind and I'm at peace. Until it happens again.

"Some might call it empathy. Identification is probably closer. I actually get out of myself and into the thing or person, and then carry it back inside me.

"I took my aunt for her regular visit to her oncologist. The people in the waiting room never read; they never talked; they just sat and stared. When I complained about the length of the wait, one said: 'Waiting is a way of life.' Waiting for what? Their sick eyes like pomegranate seeds hung in my mind until finally I got them down on paper. On canvas, the eyes saw the world through a chain of weeping DNA. Then the eyes left me alone. But I never forget."

"Sounds like you might have a special kind of insight, of understanding."

"I never sold anything. For cash, I'd put the bite on my mother, or I'd work long enough to qualify for pogey. I could always get a job, but had trouble keeping it. Something would happen and I'd be fired, or I'd quit. Even the jobs in the art field. I'd always end up leaving. I never felt comfortable. I justified leaving by saying nothing could interfere with my art."

"What happened? Why did you leave Toronto?"

"The balance, my balance, was upset. I became successful. Successful in terms of the world, that is. My art was selling as fast as I could paint it. I was besieged by women, by idiot media people. Father, of all things, became my friend, my adviser, wanting me to invest in real estate...."

"Sex, drugs, rock 'n' roll. Yeah.... And money."

"Do that dance again, Gene. You're good."

"Sorry.

"I began to drink too much, to eat too much, to smoke up too much. I preened like a pissin' peacock, sorry again, so proud. I almost stopped painting. I moved from my warehouse. The guy standing on one leg with his arms outstretched for balance now stood with his feet planted firmly on the ground. In the world's terms, a success. But I couldn't move. I couldn't paint, at least, nothing any good. I was no longer an artist, not in my eyes.

"One day, in a momentary flash of identification, I saw myself through the eyes of some broad, some smiling broad, who fleetingly dropped her smiles for a quick look of disgust. Through her opportunistic eyes, I saw this guy who thought he was so great, drinking too much booze, sniffing coke from crystal bowls through hundred-dollar bills, going to bed with cosmetically created women who read *Penthouse* for ideas, who'd laugh at any inanity, who'd do anything, any perversion, pretending it was love. I saw this guy being fawned over, his art being praised by critics, snapped up at art sales even though the recent stuff was trash.

"I suddenly saw it all as the world of money, my parents' world, the plastic world of unfeeling, and I just got up out of my water bed with its mirrored, voyeur ceiling, dug out a pair of old jeans and a sweater, and flew to Thunder Bay."

"Thunder Bay? Why would you ever want to fly to Thunder Bay? You didn't even know where it was on the map!"

"I went there because of the ships. In many of my *thinks*, boats, ships, played a big part. Me, heap-big hero. I knew it was a grain-handling port, the largest in the world, and I figured I could get a job on the boats. Although I could barely see anything, I noticed what a jumble that city is, a mish-mash of buildings I couldn't call architecture."

"But it's surrounded by incredible rock shapes.... Wonderful hourglass mountains and leaning cliffs. Cuestas. Mesas. A landscape of surreal mountains."

"To me, it was the boondocks. I'm from southern Ontario, remember? I put out the bucks to join the union, no training course was needed, and I just sat around waiting, waiting to be called. When the union room closed, I walked the waterfront, or as much as I could, since so much is industrialized."

"Didn't you see the incredible country, the Lake? Learn about the legends? There's more than a single time dimension there. The present, the obvious. And the past, the past sort of reaching out of those surreal mountains, the Sleeping Giant peninsula, a god turned to stone because his followers betrayed the secret of silver to the white man."

"Even a Judas in Indian lore."

"An Indian maid who floats in the mist over waterfalls almost as high as Niagara … or so it is said. Thunder Bay got its name because two Indian braves climbed to the nest of the sacred Thunderbird and the gods thundered their anger across the bay."

"I saw hardly anything. All I knew as I loped the waterfront was a wood-preserving plant dripping with creosote, belching paper mills, the sewage plant discharging raw crap … ah … sewage. I couldn't really see anything, understand anything. I just wanted to get on a boat."

"Just wait. Those folks up there will soon realize what they are desecrating.

"Would you believe the city has a symphony, a university, and an auditorium for world-class entertainment?"

"You're kidding."

"What do you think people do in these northern cities? Go to bed after supper?"

"Where are you from?"

"Never mind."

"I did hear there was money, an elite who, as my mother would say, could hobnob with the best."

"Gene, we're off track. Is it Thunder Bay you wanted to talk about? You're avoiding what you want to talk about."

"Jeezus, Clara. Don't push me."

"All right. All right. Don't leave. Just sit down. But remember, I don't have forever."

"Okay. Soon the word was out. Hiring was going on in Duluth, not Thunder Bay. I took a bus, crossed the border, went there. Actually, it wasn't Duluth. It was Superior. Superior, Wisconsin. Close to Duluth."

"You were hired on the *Fitzgerald*, right?"

"Well, I wasn't exactly hired."

"But I have to go. It's getting dark and you have to get your supper."

"I hope you won't walk across the Lake. I don't like that."

"I'll be okay."

§§§

At least at night with the tape recorder I can talk to you, the light of the propane lights is so unfocused I can barely read by it, let alone type, although I've almost given up typing.

I just came back from the loo. It is black-black, my flashlight giving barely enough light to guide me over the trodden path of footprints. Although those trips to the loo, like the trips to the Lake for water, get me out of the house and into the sights and sounds of the out-of-doors — no wonder people in the cities are losing touch — and although it is wonderful to get outside, I am beginning to dread those trips, especially to the loo. Never mind. On the way back tonight, waiting for the pain to ease, my focus inward, my body strung out on the snow-covered wires of the spider webs, I gradually began to notice a movement of light through the trees. It was the northern lights. Throbbing with pain but determined to let nothing slip by me, I went down to the beach. The sky and I throbbed and trembled in unison, but this time in beauty, waves of green, white, red … then a needle of white etching the black with moving peaks and spires…. Marvell…. I could have happily died right then and there.

But how would that have been for you? It might have ruined GULL ROCK for you. I will crawl away before I would let that happen.

Enough of that kind of talk. Tonight, on this wonderful night, those lights still dancing in the sky, I just want to savour you. My kids. How I enjoyed you. Oh, I was harassed with work, doing far too much drudgery for such long hours because we had so little money, Jeff still young and underpaid, and no credit was available in those days. But despite drudge and fatigue, it was impossible not to revel in you, you were so fresh, so open, so innocent of all the rottenness we are heir to.

Andrew, you had a bit of the joker in you. Like your mother. One day, I was teaching you to shake hands and say "how do you do?" Your comment: "how do you do what?"

Look, it is so cold the nailheads on the handmade wood door have frost on them. Most attractive, like a wide, studded belt.

Every time one of our friends saw you, she remembers the time we went over to her house to show her our new Labrador retriever pup, Wendigo, the dog before our German shepherd, Tasha. Like all puppies, she began to get into things and the neighbour said to you, "Call your dog, Andrew."

Do you know what you said? "Here, Andrew. Here, Andrew."

I hope when we laughed you did not think it was unkind.

And when you were ever so young and just learning to talk, your father said at dinner, "This is excellent meat."

You said, "And it's good, too."

The propane lights themselves throw warmth, their fuzzy light so warm and cozy.

You were a stalky fellow, just like your father, but able to turn seriousness into humour even at your young age. Your life in medical school has turned to raw reality, death, sleep deprivation, an overloaded brain, drained compassion, and I see the sense of humour waning. But hang on to it. Now that I examine the joking in you, I guess it wasn't all bad in me, either. Raw reality is not so nice without it. And all of us have some sort of raw reality to face.

Most of the furniture in here is antique, you know. The cranberry lamp, the Eastlake table, the trestle table made from so many kinds of wood, the cutwork-dresser scarves, old and yellowed, I wanted the place to look like it had been here forever, part of the landscape, a rabbit warren for humans, just blending in, with no intrusion to nature.

Remember when you and Clarissa were playing with a friend's child whom you didn't like? After hearing some squabbling, I went into the family room and told you both to play nicely with the visiting child. You said, "Oh, we are. We're just playing he's the bad guy, that's all."

Clarissa, what I remember most about you is your tenacity, your almost bulldog determination to grow and develop. Although I don't think we ever forget "the Nirvana of the womb" as Freud called it, there seems to be such an ambivalent impulsion to get away from it, to get away from that subliminal memory of comforting black.

How you struggled to roll over the first time. It was work, real work, and you have never forgotten that drive to work. You worked and worked to get yourself up onto your shoulder only to roll back onto your back. Finally, after a couple of days of trying, you got enough thrust to make it over onto your stomach. How you kicked and gurgled with glee.

From the day you were born you studied my mouth, gradually moulding your lips, eliminating the random sounds to finally articulate syllables both of words and of phrases. Da-Da. Da-Dee. Daddy. Pupeenicedog. Pu-pee-nice-dog. Puppy nice dog.

With you there was such an incredible thrust to develop and grow we almost became your adversaries. You seemed to feel you had to grow at our cost. It was hard on us, especially me, but I realize there must be some sort of archetypal pattern here when you think of the myths of gods that have to die so others can live.

Maybe we need new myths. New expressions of the patterns of the imagination.

Gene certainly feels antagonism towards his parents. You do, Clarissa, at least towards me. Come to think of it, I, too, completely rejected my roots and my home to find my new ones here. Growth is bought at a price. Usually when it is achieved, though, the adversity stops.

You had curly brown hair just like mine, and I can still see you marching down the street in the Indian headdress your father brought you from Toronto. It didn't matter a whit to you that you were the only one. Even if anyone made fun of you, you didn't care. Such a wonderful quality.

Reach out to me, Clarissa. You are still my little girl.

I hope you realize I really tried to be there for you when you needed me. Andrew, when your cornea was scratched in gym and you literally crawled home in pain, I was there. Clarissa, when the guy on the street tried to entice you into his car, I was there. What if I hadn't been? The public-speaking contests we worked on together, the discussions on drugs. And you had clean clothes, took vitamins, got your teeth looked after, ate good meals. With me, naturally, you ate good meals. In fact, you felt deprived because you had never tasted a TV dinner. So I bought you some.

"Give us back the beef bourguignonne, Mom," you said.

And, I did. No more TV dinners.

Only after your need for me became less did I begin the rounds of bridge games, the shopping....

I admit I was tough on you. Demanding. Expecting a lot.

Goodnight, my loves. Better find my flashlight before I turn out these propane lights. How black it is. The northern lights have gone.

JANUARY 28 · I am lying on the couch. I cannot read. I cannot clean up. I realize I am living by something I read in Sartre, something he wrote during his fight with the resistance in the last war.

He said, as well as I can remember it: "As long as I am alive, I am not dead." Well, I am still alive. Therefore I am not dead.

I think I am getting pneumonia again.

I got sick a few months after Jeff hired that secretary from New York. There was a Christmas office party. The kind to which spouses aren't invited. He was distraught and withdrawn for days. The secretary was fired, even though it left the firm short-handed.

I developed funny blotches. A strange pneumonia. And sores. Sores which kept re-appearing, everywhere.

He was very solicitous, very helpful in my search to find out what had happened to my former good health. Withdrawn, though. His way of handling difficulties.

I went down to the cave this morning, which was probably my undoing. But who cares? Earlier, when I was forced up by the demands of nature and I stumbled out in the half-light of pre-dawn to go to the loo — I am not even scared; no worry about bears now — or maybe it just doesn't matter — a fog had walled off the shore, completely obscuring the water and Gull Rock. But by the time I had breakfast and was ready to go to the cave, the fog had lifted and the scene had opened up. I could tell it was going to get colder because the northwest wind had begun to blow. The platelets of ice along the windrows of snow-ice that have created a new shoreline were still retarding the motion of the waves, giving them that slow-motion look.

The bit of wind helped clear my lungs. I was groggy with fatigue, painkillers, and brandy. I must watch the brandy. It can so easily turn from *eau de vie* to *eau de mort*.

On the shore, the snow had drifted into the soffits of the rocks. In places, it was up to my thighs as I plunged one foot in after the other. Had I been heavier, I would never have attempted it. I would never have extricated myself. Once across the drift, I would be walking on top of wind-rippled snow as easily as if I was walking on pavement.

Yes, I was in pain — but my motivation was stronger than the pain.

"Where are you going?" James Joyce was asked. "Home," he answered. "Always home." Ah … repetition. This wild, wonderful place is my home. I knew the minute I saw it, back how many years ago? I knew it was home. My early life — and the uncles — was just a stopover on my way to finding home. I am repeating again. No matter, it bears repeating. For me, anyway.

I navigated over the exposed rocks and across the wind-swept bays of fragmented lava. It is delightful to be able to manage those rocks. Why did I ever saddle myself with those thirty extra pounds. How many pounds, Clara? It was more than thirty.

When I arrived at the cave, a favourite place of everyone, it looked like a giant eye, a rounding drift of snow gazing out of the entrance like a cornea with an eyelash of icicles blinking down its forty-foot depth.

The swirling rock jowl in front of the cave was clear of snow. Just as the northwest force of the waves and wind had whirled into the molten lava of prehistoric times to create this grand jowl, this same northwest force also swept it clear.

Exhausted, I lay down in the concavity of rock. The feeling of the place came over me. I am sure it was a "magic place" for the Indians, the Ojibwa who roamed here. They would have come to the cave to contact the spirits of the other world, the manitou, because of the special feeling there.

This place is a time tunnel, backwards and forwards. Reality, the real world, seems to waiver. I ought to say that physical reality seems to waiver. For the Indians, the physical world is not the real world. The physical world is but a reflection of the real world, the Platonic world of form, the realm of the manitou. Mishipishu, the sea lynx, or water dragon, is the greatest manitou of all. Those who see Mishipishu are special and can expect special help. Imagine a rearing, spiny dragon with power radiating from its crest, plunging through the waves. This frothing dragon from another realm, one we would laugh at, was their reality.

Yet, despite the unreality of the physical world, the Indians treated it with respect. For the white man, the physical world is real, yet is exploited, dominated, and maligned. All except the physical world of money and possessions, of course.

There are so many echoes around the cave. After the Indians, the loggers came, chewing through the forest in carpenter-ant fashion. For some unexplained reason, the white pine, the oak, the red pine, and the maple that line this shore were spared. Was it because of the difficulty of logging near the rocky shore, or because some foreman felt a sense of reverence?

After the loggers, the Boy Scouts came with their shrieks of laughter, their campfires, their hidden, three-sided sleeping cabins, and their "Lake Superior screams" as they dove into its translucent cold. These boys learned about the woods, and they learned respect. When we bought the place, the forest was as clean as the Indians had left it. No pop bottles, potato-chip bags, no styrofoam cups. Ever been at the landing of a fishing camp? You should see the garbage. A black mark on the white man.

How I avoid talking to you, although I did not do badly last night. But I mean before, before I came here. I used clichés, "marvellous," brushed away your serious questions. Never really saying my thoughts like I am now. Never letting you express your inner thoughts.

Don't grieve for me. The other day I talked to you about dying in the future tense. Or did I? I can't remember. Anyway, if I did, I was wrong. I should have been talking in the present tense. You must realize that my clock of aging has speeded up; many of the systems within my body are failing. Even though I am only fifty, I am getting old. My eyes, well, you know about what has been happening to my eyes. And my memory? It is a big achievement not to forget something. Apart from the distant continent of the first twenty years of my life, my memory of the close past is collapsing like the eroding of the Kaministiquia River's sand cliffs. I stumble over the name of a familiar newscaster; I cannot remember the name of a book I just finished; or I forget a story I told an hour ago. I, who did so well at school, valedictorian, top of the class, cannot hold more than one thing in my mind at one time. Is it happening to other people of my age? If so, it is the best kept secret of the century. Too, there is the ignominy of hair growing on my face, of sagging breasts and stomach, and a neck with skin that beauticians call crepe and I call chicken skin.

Don't laugh at old people, children. Don't laugh.

As my body mechanisms go awry, as the machine begins to break down, I realize not that I am going to die, not that suddenly the angel of death will descend as our religions and mythologies wistfully lead us to believe, but I realize that as my body mechanisms go awry I will die *slowly*. The angel of death will not descend with a graceful, clean landing; but it will, in fact, surreptitiously invade like a virus — if it hasn't already — slowly taking over my body, sabotaging the mechanisms until they slowly cry to a halt. The angel of death is a succubus, an insinuating invader.

Funny, I have blotches again on my arms.

There is a difference between our body and the gradual demise of a machine. We are conscious. We feel pain. We are witness to the gradual indignities of the degenerating body, memory impairment, inability to concentrate, confusion, loss of dexterity, agility, balance, and suppleness. Have I forgotten any? The human being is totally aware that the once-bright mind, the once-adept body, is becoming laughably fuddled. Yet with head up, back bent, the degenerating individual struggles for cheerfulness and dignity.

It makes me so angry to see those young pups at the medical clinics treat old people as if they are children, calling them by their first name, smirking as they condescend to explain something, assuming that these old people have lost their ability to feel and to suffer just because they are losing their physical and mental prowess. How much a part of life dying is.

Andrew, don't you dare treat old people disrespectfully or like children. I'll come back and spank you.

I started off talking about grief. The first time I felt it was when I was six and my great grandmother died. Great Gran. My special friend. My special friend who shielded me from the teasing of my uncles. I remember the day I was told she died. I remember looking out the window. But I couldn't see. There were those glass curtains, today called sheers, obscuring my view and I was forbidden to push them aside. When I was younger and being perpetually scolded for pushing the curtains aside, I cut them off. I just took a pair of my little scissors and I cut them off. "See, Mommy, I don't have to push your curtains back anymore," I said.

When I was told about Great Gran dying, I stood at the window, but I couldn't see. What did it mean that Great Gran had died? I couldn't cry because I didn't understand. There must have been a gradual experience of grief, though, because I feel, even now, the welling up of tears.

I believe that many of our formative memories are memories of feelings only. They return to us straight, without being symbolized as words, just exactly as they were, thoughts and feelings without words. When words begin to clothe our feelings, the feelings become muted, one step removed from the power source. Metaphors. Words are just the handle of a dagger that is thrust into another reality. So many unknowns in that universe parallel to the universe we build out of words.

I still feel like that little girl standing at the window, curtains obscuring my view, wondering about death.

I hate those curtains.

I grieved for so long at the death of our dog, Wendigo. Don't laugh. You know how dogs become members of the family, just like Tasha is now. I have always been sorry, Clarissa, that you weren't there. I think you have trouble handling death. You can never run away from it. No matter where you run, it is always there looking at you. You must turn and look it straight in the eye, incorporate it into your life. It is surprising how it will change you. It might even help your relationship with me. You see, the relationship with Mother will always be there, whether I'm gone or not. I know you have been avoiding me lately, have been angry at me lately. Was it because I had begun to look sick? Maybe even old?

Don't shut me out. Even when I'm gone.

Why, look what's beside the story on the sinking of the *Fitzgerald*. Remembrance Day. Remembrance of what? All the people who died? War? Fighting against each other? Stupidity? Aren't there more important things to fight than each other? Both for and against? I feel angry at all the fighting. From my vantage point, I can certainly see the stupidity of it all. Everyone should be in my position.

Of course they are. They just don't realize it.

Or do they? And they won't admit it. Perhaps all the fighting, all the competition, all the doing is in reality a fight against the spectre of death, the opponent against whom we cannot win; therefore fight with whom you can win. Erase the spectre of final failure by winning and winning and winning and winning, in school, in tennis, in jobs, in war, in relationships.

With Jeff? Jeff with me? Did we stop fighting because he won? Because I no longer am a worthy rival for him?

For quite a while after we were married I talked with the men, usually lawyers, about politics, about the law. As I became inundated with housework, with babies, with a job that is — well, was — twenty-four hours a day, seven days a week, it wasn't long before I found myself at parties sitting on the side of the living room with the women, talking about babies and shopping.

Life for women is better now. Mothers have more support systems like exercise classes and day care and a realization by men that male participation with the children is important.

It was mainly you kids that Jeff and I fought about. He treated you like he treated himself. Especially you, Andrew. When he saw his own failings in you — windmill eating, enthusiasm that verged on impatience, forgetfulness about personal grooming, working to the point of exhaustion, and crabbiness — he sort of went berserk. Instead of trying to correct his example, he tried to correct you, his mirror image, an impossibility, of course. He was tough, demanding, almost trying to pummel you into what he wanted of himself. He was hard on himself, too. When this self-hate became too vigorous, he would reward himself, or you, with a gift of money, or an indulgence of food. Food is love with the Ukrainians. Your father had to fight to stay even moderately slim because of his constant need to give himself food, not only to survive but to gratify.

Odd, I never before recognized the similarity in our personality. We both ate to try to overcome our self-hate. I never realized that before.

Me and my feeds. Why, when you think of it, I looked like a piggie, fuzzy white-blond hair, pink and white and soft....

If only you knew how we fought and argued about you behind closed doors. Probably you did know. Kids know more than their parents give them credit for. Your father's impatience with you was the main point of contention in our married life. That and my brains. However, housework, fashion and my joking took care of my brains.

Perhaps luckily for me and the family, I was a fairly compliant, non-aggressive individual. Your father was always geared to fight. His livelihood, the courtroom lawyer, depended on his adeptness in the duel. Compassion, fairness, equanimity were not in his arsenal of tools. I often thought that he should have married Elizabeth, not me. She would have given him more colour, more duelling. She would have been more like the Ukrainian matriarchs he was used to.

How can you be of Ukrainian extraction with a name like Wheatley? Wheatley came from Pszenyczny, which somebody at Immigration changed when your grandfather arrived in Canada. But I've told you all that, haven't I?

"Many times, Mother. Many times."

Somehow Elizabeth escaped the patriarchy of our background, and of society. She scoffed at our brother getting the heirloom gold cane and the family archives. She scoffed at him being "head" of the family when Dad died. I didn't. I just accepted.

Until now. No more.

Like you, Andrew.

After you were in the automobile accident, Andrew; after you experienced the searing of pain, the touch of death from fatty embolisms lurking in your arteries, you got up from that hospital bed and never fought with your father again. Your eyes, previously wild like Gene's, settled down. You declared you would not be a lawyer, that you would be a doctor. Your individuality established, the stand off was accepted.

Clarissa, your rejection of me is a tie like dependency is. On your own two feet, simply accepting your parents as they are, as I am, you could be free. Simply accepting death, my death, you can be free. If you forever fight against it, against me, you will not be free of either.

All this is so complex. Rejection. Acceptance.

Better get back to being philosophical.... What was I saying? Winning? Harm? Oh yes, how much harm, evil really, results from this perpetual search to win from this displaced fear of death?

If death were just accepted as part of life, not an antithesis of it, perhaps much of the fighting in the world would stop.

How much of life is death?

How much of death is life?

You can't have one without the other. That song again.

They seem to be different facets of a root motivation and yet we have no name for it. Life and death is really an array of colour like the spectrum, yet we have no name for the life-death spectrum. Perhaps *vita-mors*.

As a spectrum, society and doctors would necessarily come to understand how to deal with the union of both polarities, and especially with the only certainty anyone has in life. You got it. Not taxes. Death.

I know I have read these ideas somewhere. Was it Becker? No matter. They are mine now. I have incorporated them into my thinking, my point of view. Yet I have never discussed any of this with you, with anyone.

I can hear the walls shouting: "Don't be so serious, Chubby. Don't be so serious."

To hell with you, uncles.

I can still see Andrew carrying that big, limp, black retriever to her grave, her legs almost dragging on the ground, he being so careful, so gentle. Andrew and your father dug that grave through rocks and roots during a pelting rainstorm. Neither wanted to leave her at the vet's to be thrown in the dump in a garbage bag. They dug her grave just out there while the dog rested on the back seat of the car, dead. Her arthritis had reached the point where she could hardly walk. There was no complaining, no crying, just the brown eyes always looking at us with gratefulness in them. It was a unanimous family decision that she should be put to sleep. Clarissa, do I remember correctly that you would not take part in the discussion? Anyway, the morning we took her to the vet, she just seemed to know. She struggled out of the house and climbed onto the back seat of the car. We drove her to the vet's and he came outside with his long needle poised, Andrew giving a big sob, I sort of holding her. She lay there majestically with her head up, the needle in her elbow for what seemed the longest time, and then she slowly, very naturally, just put her head down on her paws and died. It was so peaceful, so natural, a beautiful death.

Is that an oxymoron, the coupling of two contradictory terms? Beautiful death. I cried many times afterwards. I am crying now.

But her planned death was so kind, so humane, if indeed a word derivative of human can mean kind. Humans are so cruel. She went to sleep with her loved ones around her, totally trusting their judgment. Why are we kinder to our pets, some of us are, than to our fellow human beings? Her loved ones had set the terms of her death and it was the best possible.

Because you cannot legally share the terms of my death with me, I realize I must set them myself.

Ahead of me lies only pain and suffering; ahead of you would lie only mute horror as you watch me die. It won't be a kindly and loving death. It will be a draining, alienating, fruitless experience for everyone. I had a taste of what it would be like when I had that terrible pneumonia, the illness that started all this chain of illnesses. I saw you pale and worried by my bedside. Even you, Clarissa. Thank you for coming. I only wish you could be with me, just like we were with Wendigo. Someday it will be so. Right now, in order to set the terms of my own death, I must die alone. You will all be with me in my thoughts.

What you must realize, despite what society says, is that some suicide is rational — self-euthanasia — and if I do say so, brave. The carefully considered decision to sign myself out of the hospital, to stop wasting everyone's money, to drag myself here, was difficult. How much easier to give up? To let myself lapse into animal pain, to give myself over to drugs, to lose my identity and eventually die, a non-entity.

No. I want to die as Clara Wheatley, strong, peaceful, rational, with you in my thoughts.

Most of all, I want to die on my own terms.

Don't worry. I am still clinging to life, despite the pain, despite the difficulty of living. I am still savouring being alive. Gene is actually giving me a bit more time. My curiosity in his story is making me hang on. And he is making it easier for me. He carries the water, brings in the wood, gets the provisions out of the root cellar.

I think I'll pop a little brandy and make a nice supper. Brandy is more fun than those damn pain- and mind-killers. Now how about seafood crepes and crème caramel for a nice wilderness dinner? Oh yes, I forgot to tell you. Gene is going to move in.

JANUARY 29 · I told you yesterday—or was it the day before?—about the heavy embroidery of ice called brash that had formed out of round ice platelets bobbing near the perimeter of the Lake. I did, didn't I?

This ice embroidery is the widest and thickest in the unfrozen bays and coves; and it describes tantalizing patterns as it eddies outward on the gyre of the Lake current. When the swells of the Lake undulate into the lace, they move in a heavy motion as if the Lake had entered another reality.

This morning after a drop both in temperature and wind, the Lake indeed moved into another reality, the eternal frozen world where time seems to have stopped, if it ever does. Here, anything that seems to be life, me, Gene, a bird, a sound, is an intruder.

But what a prelude there was to this stillness, this eternity. It was a grand Wagnerian prelude that began last night.

I actually heard the Lake freeze up.

"Mother," you say. "How could you hear the Lake freeze up?"

Well, I did.

It began last night when I stepped out onto the veranda to begin my nightly perambulation to the loo, the sound from the Lake seemed to come through a giant stethoscope pulsing from somewhere near Gull Rock. As this sound travelled across the water to the shore, I thought I was losing my mind.

I called Gene. He helped me down to the water's edge. There, close to the Lake, not only did we hear the pulsing, we heard other pitches of sound, clatters, raspings, and tinkles. The Lake was virtually speaking.

Behind the forest, the moon was rising. Its white light was caught on shore by something I couldn't quite identify. It framed a delicate necklace of light around the shore.

With difficulty, I went to bed, awakening this morning again to the sounds of the ice. I struggled out. There was the white opaqueness of motionless ice as far as the eye could see — and lining the shore and angling across to the mound of ice that was Gull Rock were panes of ice as transparent and geometric as glass. They must have been broken from the flat of the freezing Lake and neatly stacked by the swells into sheaves. The stethoscopic sound I heard last night must have reverberated along this ridge.

I stood and listened to the heaving and rasping of the Lake.

Then, there was a rolling wail.

All sound stopped.

Lake Superior had frozen over.

As I walked back to the cottage, I heard the occasional gurgle or rattle — but essentially it seemed the world had stopped.

I wish you could have heard it, my Andrew, my Clarissa. I wish you could have been here with me to hear it. It was unique, so personal, so prescient. There seemed to be no demarcation between what was inside me and what was outside; everything was perception, my perception — which, of course, it always is — but usually we are not so aware of it. Again, I suspect repetition. If Gene hadn't been there at least part of the time, I am not sure I would have believed it happened. Gene was there. I am certain he was there.

"I see you're hard at it on the tape recorder."

"Yes. I still have things to say to my children, to myself. Yet I don't seem to be saying them."

"Did you eat yet?"

"I think I'll forget breakfast. Want to get going on your story?"

"Do you mind if I get something? Make some coffee?"

"Of course not. I apologize for thinking only of myself."

What's happening to me? I am shrinking into myself. You know how life is a flowering, a reaching, a reaching outward? Well, death is a retreat, a shrinking, a withering. I am determined, however, that despite my withering and shrinking inward, what happens to me will be proud and individual and lovely....

"Shrinking? Withering? What are you talking about?"

"I didn't hear you come into the room. Will you pass me that bottle of pills in the armoire over there?"

"Why are you taking pills?"

"Just you never mind."

"I'll get you some water."

"Forget the water. Get me some brandy."

"I don't know about that, Clara. It can't be good for you. Before breakfast? On an empty stomach? Booze and drugs?"

"Believe me, Gene, at my stage of life, it's okay."

"If you say so."

"Here you are. I guess I'll smash a little brandy in my coffee, too, although the sun isn't over the yardarm yet."

"It is for me."

"Pardon?"

"Again, never mind."

"Now where was it I left off?"

"You're asking me? You were somewhere, Duluth, I think. No Superior, Superior, Wisconsin."

"Oh, yes. You were right. I did board the *Big Fitz*, 'the pride of the flag.' Did you know she was the biggest ship on the Great Lakes until just four years ago? A friggin' floatin' bathtub, technically called a straight-decker?"

"I read she was supreme for some thirteen years."

"I boarded her, but I wasn't exactly hired.

"I am a bit ashamed to say that I sneaked on her. Despite the rumours about hiring goin' on at Duluth and Superior, they weren't hiring. Nothin' was goin' down.

"Then, one sunny day, in my travels around the waterfront, I saw a guy laboriously unloading boxes from a truck parked on the ore dock by the *Edmund Fitzgerald*.

" 'Need help?' I asked.

" 'I sure do,' he answered. 'My partner is friggin' sick and I have to get these fuck....'

"Clara, the language, I'm sorry ... but it's part of the story.... That's the way those men talk."

"Just censor it, that's all. Or forget it. My ears aren't garbage cans."

"Jeeze...."

"And censor your own language, too. Swearing is nothing but laziness."

"Jeeze.... Anyway, this guy said he had to get the boxes on the *Fitz* because it was pulling out after noon.

"He hired me on the spot. I hid my backpack on the loading platform where we were piling the boxes. When we were finished and he paid me, I went back on board to supposedly retrieve my jacket, and I never got off.

"I hid in a dunnage room. It was hot, stuffy, uncomfortable, and noisy. The sounds from the loading of the taconite...."

"What?"

"Taconite, the cargo, little balls of iron like dog kibble. They thundered into the hold through oblong hatches that ribbed the open deck. There was also the noise of the boat shunting as it moved under another chute, the consecutive clanging of the hatch covers by the hatch crane, and finally the incessant hammering that went on all around each hatch. What a din. Bloody ... ah ... pretty important, though, especially the hammering of the hatch covers."

"Why?"

"If the hatches aren't securely closed in a storm, water could get in."

"Oh."

"Under way, the din of the hatch-hammering continued. I could find nothing comfortable to curl up on; there were only piles of lumber and grates. I finally sat against my knapsack in a corner and waited. I certainly did not want to be discovered until we were well away from port.

"I had tried to foresee all contingencies. In my backpack, I had food, warm clothes, a wetsuit, life vest, even a few beer.

"A couple of beer out of port, and I was caught. The need for a pi ... a bathroom, or head, as it's called on a ship, undid me.

"I was pushed into the crew's quarters and they had their fun at my expense.

" 'What kinda motherfu.... What ... ah ... do we have here?' "

"I don't have earlids, Gene."

"After many ... ah ... obscene suggestions, they decided I was a stowaway.

" 'Throw him in the hold. He can have fun with himself in the dark.'

" 'That's what's done with stowaways, you know.'

" 'Naw. Hang him by his.... '

" 'Put him in irons.'

" 'Better take him to the Old Man.' "

"Who?"

"The Old Man. The Captain. The Master. Ernest M. McSorley.

"I didn't want to be taken to him yet. I might be pitched off somewhere. I really wanted this trip, something fresh to clear my mind. I pleaded with them. I'd give them money. I'd work.

"You have to admit, Clara, I can be a brown nose ... ah ... pleasing and persuasive when I want to."

"As long as you don't swear."

"With those men, swearing was their language.

"One of the crew said: 'Yeah. Better wait. The Old Man's on the radio about some sh … awful weather coming up from Kansas.'

"'I hear he's been talkin' to the *Arthur M. Anderson*. She's just behind us.'

"A little time was all I needed. When the bad weather hit, the crew forgot about me. By seven o'clock, we were in ten-foot waves. No expletives in my mind now. Those waves were art, Gainsborough ruffles of white on sleeves of blue…."

"See? You can express yourself."

"Anyway, I was on a high. I went around looking at the sea, at the *Fitz*, a sleek leviathan of industry, its belly engorged with cargo, cutting through those sleeves of blue, spraying out its own white ruffles of foam. I exulted in the human handiwork, the ship's invincibility.

"'Hey, Cunty Kid….'"

"Gene!"

"I'm sorry. That's what they called me."

"If you were telling the story to your mother would you use that word?"

"Of course not. But I wouldn't tell the story to my mother. And, you're not my mother. In fact, I was thinking of asking you if you'd like … well … to go to bed with me."

"What? You've got to be joking."

"Clara! I'm not that bad, am I? You're going to give me an inferiority complex."

"You're very nice, very charming. I'm flattered. I really am. It's just … well … very ironic what you have suggested, that's all."

"Why?"

"Never mind. Think of it this way: an affair would complicate things. More than you would ever want. Besides, we need each other for other reasons, remember?"

"Hell. Whistler's whelp!"

"What?"

"Whistler's whelp? My own personal expletive. Confuses people."

"It does."

"But you're avoiding the subject. Maybe I won't give up. We could have a, well, nice relationship."

"You had better give up, believe me. If you only knew, knew what I suspect but will never know."

"What are you talking about?"

"Just get on with your story, will you? You're looking for excuses to get out of talking about what's bothering you. And when you say what the men called you, just say Kid."

"Anyway, they told me to get to work.

"As I worked, careful to keep away from anyone in authority, my mind never shut up. I realized I didn't have to be a victim of those bloody media parasites in Toronto. I didn't have to let others dictate my life. I told myself to grow up. I didn't have to be slotted by the materialism I didn't want, those brainless pornographic women. But the thought was only nosing out like a car into traffic. Soon there were other concerns.

"It had been a clear, beautiful day when we sailed into the beak and up the throat of Lake Superior, to use your bird image, Clara. But soon we hit the masticating, stormy jaws."

"You can be quite articulate when you quit the swearing."

"It takes longer."

"But you're saying something. Not just grunting."

"Anyway, not only was there a storm, there was snow. Someone heard there were gale warnings.

" 'Hey, Cu … Kid, this isn't bad.'

" 'Hey, Kid. You seasick?'

"But I wasn't. I had never been seasick, never, no matter how rough it had been when I was out sailing on my father's yacht.

" 'You scared?'

"Scared? I had entered the world of art, the matter of art, so elemental and internal was my experience. The trivia of the world was gone. The superfluous was gone. I was now on the prow of that ship, working, doing, being. The tensions in my mind disappeared.

"What I didn't know was that new ones would develop.

"During the night, there was the roar of the waves, the thud of the big ones. I was told the gale warnings had been changed to storm warnings, which I knew meant very heavy weather, big winds. I was also told that both the *Fitz* and the *Anderson* had changed course away from the main shipping channel. In order to be in the lee of the shore, they were going to take the northern route along the north shore of Lake Superior. The trip would take longer, but what did I care?

"In the early morning, after an uncomfortable night in the dunnage room and a breakfast of granola bars and beer, I was discovered by the first mate, some guy by the name of McCarthy.

" 'You're coming with me to the pilot house to see the Old Man. Storm or no storm.' "

"Did they put you in chains?"

"This time there was no fooling.

"The ship was rolling from side to side and even with my agility I found it difficult climbing the stairs to the pilot house.

" 'Lookit what kinda piece a sh ... I found,' the first mate said.

"The Old Man, looking every inch a captain even without his nautical blue, glared at me and turned away.

" 'I just got off of the radio to the company in Detroit to say we'd be late arriving at the Sault locks because of the weather. I wish I'd known about this other problem sooner.'

"He was referring to me.

" 'I just found him,' the first mate said, 'although the crew musta known.'

" 'When things settle down a bit, I'll call and report a stowaway.'

"I never knew if he made that call. Later I found out he didn't.

"Around noon, the nor'easter— 'learn the language, Kid'— was subsiding.

" 'It probably means a wind shift, Kid.'

" 'It's gunna haul ta the nor'west, you'll see.'

"I could see a change in the crew. They were quieter. The jokes, mostly at my expense, were fewer. They just sat and watched TV, such as it was. Mostly they looked at their watch or asked about the time.

" 'What time is it?'

" 'Fourteen-ten.'

" 'Go git in yur bunk, Kid. If you're scared. That's all you can do.'

"I didn't have a bunk and I wasn't scared.

" 'What time is it, Kid, on that expensive watch of yours?'

" 'It's fourteen-twenty,' someone shouted.

" 'This sure is a long trip.' "

"Does anyone know where the love of God goes when the waves turn the minutes to hours?"

"What?"

"From Gordon Lightfoot's song. You shouldn't say 'what.' "

"Clara! I'm not a child. Besides, you said 'what' a couple of times. Not very ladylike."

"Don't say that."

"We followed the steep wall of rock that seemed to be much of the north shore of Lake Superior, the waves oddly splashing shoreward, sending white spray upwards into the darkness of the day as they crashed into the towering peninsulas of rock that is the crown of Lake Superior. The *Anderson* was behind and farther out, cutting corners to keep up with the faster *Fitz*.

"For a while I thought there was a lull.

" 'The nor'wester's not subsiding, Kid. It's just bidin' it's time.' "

"How big were the waves?"

"Ten, twenty feet. I was to learn it wasn't bad yet."

"How did you ever get off?"

"Did you hear that?"

"It sounds like a dog ... and a snowmobile."

"Jeezuschris. There is someone outside. Again. Here's where I disappear. Just give me a minute before you answer the door."

"It's Jeff."

"I'm leaving."

"Jeff!

"And Tasha. Dear Tasha. You're so glad to see me."

"Clara, I've come to take you home."

JANUARY 30 · It is the end of January, I think. I fell today when I went down to get water from the Lake. Although Jeff had left all four buckets full, I was obsessed to go and fill the empty ones, even on this cold January day, the wind whining across the ice, snow devils dancing on the wind-pressed beach.

With the buckets dragging behind me, I crawled up and over the slippery windrow of weathered ice sheaves that curves around my little inlet. I pushed back my marker and plywood covering for the waterhole. After dipping my pail into the silvery water, I struggled to my feet. With the wind gusting at my back, I involuntarily ran up and over the windrow. And I fell. The water splashed into my boots, onto my legs. When I fell, I was cut with the pain of the ice water, and torn apart by my other pain. I howled like a wounded dog — such ignominy — like a wailing banshee. I collapsed backwards with my eyes closed for the longest time, tears freezing on my cheeks. I looked up into the sky. The mare's tail clouds swished, slowing in anger against the deceiving blue. I looked past the angry tails into the peaceful, unending sky. I seemed to move up into it, ever so easily, ever so slowly. Somehow in a powerful thrust of will, not ready yet to sleep, I got up and made it back to the cabin, my slacks frozen almost like casts on my legs.

Here I sit, dripping onto the floor.

Gene has not come back yet after his fright at seeing your father. I certainly will need his help. I have left it too long. I will never get out of here alone. You see, I must leave this place unsullied for you. I want it to remain pristine and beautiful. No garbage.

I am beginning to worry about Gene's legal involvement. I must not tell him my plan, only part of it.

I sit here looking at the mousetraps. They have mice in them. I know their sightless black eyes are staring upwards, the killing bar of the trap hidden benignly in the folds of their neck. At least they died quickly and painlessly. I wish I could get up to remove their inert forms from my sight. Death at its best is not easy.

There is garbage in the kitchen. Although Jeff cleaned up everything before he left, garbage always develops. Was it only yesterday Jeff left? Or the day before?

If Gene comes back—oh, Gene, you must come back—when he comes back, I will have him consolidate all the garbage in tight pails in the boathouse. It will freeze and shouldn't attract animals before you get a chance to empty it. I don't want to leave a mess for you.

Maybe Jeff took the garbage. I am losing track of things.

I would just like to sleep....

§§§

"Clara? What are you doing sitting in a chair in wet clothes?"

"I fell."

"Holy sh.... The fire's almost out."

"It is?"

"I'm going to have to rebuild it."

"Where are you going?"

"To get you some dry clothes."

"Get something easy to put on. Get some of Jeff's clothes.

They're in the closet."

I can hear him rummaging around in the closet looking for clothes. I am so glad he came back.

"Here they are. I'll hold up this blanket as a screen. You get changed behind it.

"Maybe I should build the fire first. Or tea. Wait, I'll put the kettle on.

"There. The kettle's on. Clara, you're shaking. Gotta get you outta those clothes."

"No, you don't."

"Here. I got you a towel to dry yourself."

"Hold that blanket up, will you? No peeking."

"I won't."

"It's hard getting these clothes off when they're wet."

"Just take your time."

"Okay. Finally. That feels better."

"Now just lie down on the chesterfield and I'll put this blanket over you."

"No, I'll sit on a chair, a dry chair, by the fire. Yes, give me that blanket. And give me some brandy."

"Brandy's not good for you when you're cold."

"Gene, forgawdsake. Now I'm swearing."

"Right. But you're a strange lady. I don't know how you think you're going to get out of here unless you look after yourself."

You don't, eh?

"Now that's better. What a lovely trickling of warmth as it goes down. Is the tape recorder on?"

"Yes, it's on."

§§§

"Gene? What are you doing now? Will you get in here and finish your story?"

"You were sleeping. I was just hanging up your wet clothes."

"I'm not sleeping now. I want you to finish your story. We have to go somewhere. I have to do something.

"Is the tape recorder going?"

"Let me look again. Yes, it's going."

"Good."

"Wouldn't you like some tea?"

"Tea? I'm past tea. You know what I like."

"Okay. Where's the brandy?"

"Now let's go."

"Where was I?"

"Don't ask me."

"The pitch of the storm was increasing. Lake Superior felt like a sea, an ocean. But the waves didn't behave like those of the seas or oceans I have known, or like the oceans you see on TV. The waves didn't furrow the water regularly. Some were close together, some far apart, some so far apart that at times the Lake almost seemed calm. Then the waves would build up, raking the ship with water. They were like animals, breathing foam at us, rearing up and plunging over the ship."

"Because you dared confront the storm."

"Wild, legendary beasts pursuing a ship. The *Fitzgerald* no longer 'the pride of the flag,' seven hundred and twenty-nine feet of steel and usefulness, a sleek leviathan.

"The *Fitzgerald* had been transformed by that storm into a soggy log. It would roll over so far it felt like it would never come back, and then it would slowly roll the other way.

"The Old Man, the Captain, he said the ship was 'rolling some.'"

"He was not given to exaggeration."

"He certainly wasn't.

"I was told we were passing an island. Caribou Island."

"Caribou Island? The one near Thunder Bay?"

"No. The one I mean is just a little island with a big shoal, can't be too far from here, somewhere in the easterly end of the Lake.

"Although it was the middle of the afternoon by now and we were passing close to the starboard side, the waves and the snow stopped us from seeing it. The frenzy of the storm was increasing. The noise! We no longer heard the ship's roar of aggression, we only heard the ship's scream of pain. We were living in a scream. The sound never abated.

"I could feel the tension of the men. I could feel my own tension. My thinking was forced to turn an ugly corner. Could I possibly be in danger?

"Then I felt something: a hard, unforgiving smack.

" 'We hit bottom. Didn't you feel it?' I shouted to one guy.

" 'Kid, we didn't. It was just her smackin' the bottom of a wave, that's all.'

" 'The Old Man would a never let her touch, Kid. Never.'

" 'You're wrong,' I shouted. 'She hit.'

" 'Lookit, if them charts are right, Old Man McSorley would'a never hit bottom. He's good. He has forty-four years' experience under his belt.'

"In the corridor on the way to the head—I seemed to be going a lot—I stopped one of the crew.

" 'This ship has electronic devices and gauges to tell the depth, doesn't it?' I asked.

" 'Course not, Kid. Gettin' worried, are you? As well you should. This state-of-the-art ship only has a hand lead. Wanna throw it overboard to test the depth, do you? She ain't got no fathometer or depth-sounder, no siree.'

"I told him I couldn't believe it. Even my father's yacht had an echo-sounder. I wasn't sure if he was kidding me or telling the truth.

"It wasn't long after that I noticed the ship was listing. It was sort of lying over to one side like a fish does when it's dying. There was some hushed talk of damage, some whispers of water in the ballast tanks.

"'Nothin', Kid. Just lost some guard rail and vent covers. Nothin' to worry about. Besides, there's no point in worryin' now.'

"I heard someone say: 'The radar's out.'

"'The radar's out?'

"'Don't worry, Kid. The *Anderson*'s sendin' us our position. The Old Man's slowin' down to let her catch up.'

"'And the radio beacon is out at Whitefish Point?'

"'The light is out there, too?'

"Can you imagine, Clara, the *Fitzgerald* caught in the maw of such a fierce storm and all her support systems gone? Only the *Anderson* behind trying to guide her?"

"It was lack of respect for the Lake, that's all I can say.

"I think I'll sit on the chesterfield. How about a little more of you-know-what?"

"Okay."

"We can see that light on Whitefish Point in the summer. Not now, not in winter. The horizon seems dead without it. Even the gulls...."

"The waves were swirling over the slanted deck. We seemed so low in the water.

"'She is low, Kid. They raised the load line by more than three feet from when she was first built back in 1958. She just sits low now, that's all.'

"It was the same guy who told me there was no depth-sounder. Was he kidding me again?

"Over in the corner, I could hear some men saying that the Mackinaw Bridge had been closed, that the locks in the Sault had been shut down, and that the lock master said the winds were ninety-five miles an hour. Even the Old Man said it was one of the worst seas he'd ever seen.

" 'If you wanted to see if there's water in the hold, how would you do it?' I asked.

" 'Will ya get that kid outta here?' someone shouted.

" 'Yeah. He's talkin' too much.'

" 'Give him somethin' to do.'

" 'Yeah. Just shut him up.'

" 'Here, Kid. Take this here book to the chief engineer. Let's see what you're made of.'

" 'Yeah, and let's see if you can put down some dinner while you're at it.'

" 'If the cook can make dinner, that is.'

" 'Sure, I'll take the book. And sure, I can eat,' I said.

"I ducked into the dunnage room and put on my wetsuit and life vest. I put my jeans and jacket back on, stuffed rope and food bars into my pockets and attached a flashlight and knife to my belt. I had learned one good thing from my father: be prepared when you're on the water."

"You only learned *one* good thing from your father? Poor fathers. Poor parents...."

"I thought, 'to hell with the philosophy of these guys.' I wasn't going to lie down. Even if I had a bunk I wasn't going to get in it.

"As I passed the lounge, I shouted: 'Are you sure there's no way to tell if there's water in the hold?'

" 'Kid, there's no instrument or gauge, if that's what you mean.'

" 'There are ways to get in, but who could see?'

" 'The water could be two inches below those pellets and you'd never know it.'

" 'Forgit it, will ya?'

"I asked: 'What about those tanks I hear you talking about, those ballast tanks?'

" 'Them compartments have gauges that register in the pilot house. The Old Man would know if there was water in them. In fact, there is. He's got the pumps goin' now.'

" 'Don't tell him that. He's scared enough now.'

" 'It's just a November storm, Kid. No ship has sank on Lake Superior for some twenty-two years. Will you just shut up?'

" 'Hey, lookit what he's got on,' someone shouted.

" 'Come over by the light, Kid. Let's see what you're wearin'.'

"They opened my jacket and pulled up my jeans. And they had a good laugh.

" 'A wetsuit.'

" 'You don't say.'

" 'Gettin scared, are ya?'

" 'I'm taking this book to the engine room now,' I said. 'And I'm going to get dinner, too.'

"As I left, I could hear howls of laughter. I didn't think it was that funny.

"There, I got through all that and you didn't hear one swear word, did you, Clara?"

"I think I will lie down."

"I was laughing with the men as I ducked out of the lounge. However, once facing the deserted companionways of the forward deckhouse, I lost the smile on my face. I clung to the steel railing of a steep, scary stairway and inched my way down. At the bottom, inside the tunnel that runs lengthwise down the ship, I felt fear, real mind-destroying fear. The tunnel was a spider web of steel angles, a surreal perspective of infinite squares that seemed to disappear into each other. What was I doing in this nightmare perspective? How could this web, supposedly a ramrod of bolts and steel, resist the stresses that were pursuing it? Here, the sound was not a scream; it was a low, vibrating groan. I moved into the sound, canting, staggering, clinging to whatever I could. How long it took me to traverse the treadmill length of the tunnel I don't know, but I sure was happy to see the steep, scary stairway up to the aft deckhouse. Before I began the long climb up the stairs, I bent down and put my ear to the deck plates. I swore I could hear the water sloshing underneath. I climbed those stairs two at a time despite the rolling of the ship, and I finally found the engine room.

"Then I stopped. I felt it, a sort of slithering of the ship. Strange.

"I handed the book to the engineer and asked: 'Do you think there's water in the hold? And what's that strange feeling in the ship, sort of like an eel?'

" 'The Captain calls it 'the wiggling thing.' Yeah, he said he was scared of it.'

" 'You mean there might be something wrong with the ship, the hull?'

" 'What does it matter, Kid? There's nothin' we can do.'

" 'Git outta here, will ya? Just git outta here.'

" 'Who is he, anyway?'

" 'Must be that stowaway.'

" 'Just get him outta here.'

"I left and began to look around. The mess was deserted. There was no sign of the cook. In the crew's quarters, men were curled up in their bunks and appeared to be sleeping.

" 'Git outta here.'

"They sounded like they would kill me.

"I went where I could see the spar deck, the open deck. It was dark, but in the shadows of the ship's lights, or in the light of my imagination, I am not sure which, I could see the rows of parallel hatches that looked like rows of huge coffins, coffins for the iron pellets that had been loaded at Superior. And I could see the toad-stool field of caps, or what the crew called vents, vents into the ballast tanks and the tunnels.

"When a wave reared over the deck, the water swirled around these projections creating rivers and eddies and currents.

"Then I saw a toadstool cap was missing! Water had to be going down that open pipe!

"I searched the deck to see if there were more problems. Were those damn coffin-shaped hatches closed? I couldn't tell.

"But the vent, I could tell about the vent. Water was going down!

"I think I went berserk. For the first time in my life, I felt terror. My mind was moving at the speed of light, but everything around me had slowed down, the ship rolled over on its side and seemed to stay there. Gradually it would right itself. The water slid over the cambered deck and ever so cunningly searched out openings. Colour had blanched. Everything was reverse black and white like the negative of a photograph. The storm and the sea had substance; the ship was an absence, a nothing. I was in the world of abstract art. Everything was shape and form and elemental design etched into a background of black. I didn't like it. My mind was saying, 'Re-create this scene. It's not right. Go back and do it again.'

"But this was no *think*, no fantasy, no canvas I was painting on. No matter how I tried, nothing would change.

"And then I began a litany in my mind. It still is a litany in my mind.

" 'Gotta tell the Captain.'

" 'Gotta tell the Captain.' "

"Everybody's got litanies in their mind."

"Clara? What did you say?"

"Nothing."

"I didn't feel right calling him, the Old Man.

"I ran around looking for a phone. Was there a phone? They must communicate some way. I'd heard the crew talking about a public-address substation. Why hadn't I paid attention?

"I ran back to the engine room.

" 'There's water, water going down a vent. And I heard water in the hold. I heard it,' I screamed. 'Phone the Captain. If you don't believe me, come and look. Will you? Will you come and listen?'

"Do you know what they said?

" 'Git outta here, Cunty Kid. Just git outta here.'

" 'The Old Man already knows some vent covers are missing.'

"I realized I had heard that before.

" 'What about the water?' I said.

" 'Ferchrissake! Git!'

"I began to run around again. No point in trying to wake the sleeping men. They'd kill me. I found myself at the top of another endless flight of steep, scary stairs that led to the access tunnel along the other side of the ship. If I was going to tell the Captain, I would have to go down into that web of steel surrealism again. Scared as I was, I went. 'Gotta tell the Captain.' I inched down the stairs. At the bottom, when I opened the door to the tunnel—oh my god—I saw water. Jeezus, I saw water in the tunnel!

"I climbed back up those stairs like a monkey chased by a forest fire. At the top my heart was pounding, but I wasn't tired. Those stairs were the height of a tall building, but I wasn't tired.

"I started to run again. I had to make someone listen.

" 'Gotta tell the Captain.'

"I looked out a porthole to see what was happening to the storm. As if I didn't know, as if I couldn't feel the sickening roll as the ship heeled over farther and farther and farther and then ever so slowly righted itself only to go over farther and farther and farther on the other side, all this slow-motion action accompanied by the moaning of pain. Was it rolling or had it begun to tip back and forth like a rocking horse? I can't remember."

"Memory is faulty. Especially under stress."

"Clara. I can hardly hear you.

"Then I saw it! Holy shit! On the open deck, a lifeboat. Painted on the side was: EDMUND FITZGERALD, NUMBER 2, FIVE HUNDRED CUBIC FEET. FIFTY PERSONS. Capital letters."

"It's strange, the details you remember."

"She didn't even notice I was swearing."

" 'Forget it,' I said to myself as I thought about jumping in the lifeboat.

" 'Gotta tell the Captain.'

"As I was passing the door to the open deck where I'd seen the lifeboat, a big wave hit. Did it hit from a different direction? Had the wind backed around again? And I swear, I swear, I heard that cargo of black iron balls move. They slid like the sound of pebbles on a beach as a wave recedes. In what was left of my rational mind, I doubted I could actually have heard the cargo move over the sound of the storm. But I wasn't listening to my rational mind. When I regained my balance from the jolt of the wave, I braced myself for the next — but it didn't come. There was one of those mysterious Lake Superior lulls."

"What did you do?"

"Pardon? Clara? I forgot about.... I didn't hear what you...."

"What did you do?"

"I am so ashamed. After all my dreams, after all my *thinks* and imaginings, there I was, in the position to save a crew. There I was, actually in one of my fantasies. I had the knowledge to be a hero, to save lives. What did I do? Did I go back down those long stairs and wade through that watery tunnel forward to the pilothouse and the Captain? Did I?

"No. I didn't.

"I flung open the door to the deck. In the lull of the waves, I scrambled into the lifeboat, slashing through the canvas with my knife and falling into the boat before the next wave struck. I clung for my life to the thwart because this wave was even bigger than the last. Again I had the feeling the wind had changed direction. In fact, the ship seemed to be circled by giant waves coming at it from everywhere, a maelstrom....

"The ship shuddered. I pulled out my rope and I lashed myself to the thwart. I lashed myself as tightly as I could to that seat.

"With the next wave, the *Big Fitz* went down. Over the roar of the waves, I heard the cargo surge to the front — how could I hear it? — and the bow plunged into the sea. The next thing I knew, I was choking, coughing, gasping for air—and floating on the sea in a lifeboat. It had broken free.

"I remember hearing planes over the roar of the waves. There was a fantasy of strobe lights, but I wasn't sure if it was in my head or out there. Maybe it was flares or searchlights, I don't know. Later, much later, I got my head up and I thought I could see a ship. It looked like the *Anderson,* but again I really couldn't tell. I floated and I floated for how long, I really don't know. I thought I was going to freeze to death. I was shivering. My legs and arms were so cold they felt like they were burning. Isn't that weird? I was freezing to death and I felt like I was on fire. Although I was lying still, my heart was pounding into the seat. I could hear the pounding of my heart more than I could hear the pounding of the waves. I began to dream of big birds rescuing me, but as they swooped down to pluck me out of the sea they saw who it was and they veered away. I struggled against the rope tied around my waist—'Gotta tell the Captain'—and I kept mumbling and yelling and trying to get loose. But I was too weak. When I moved I remember hearing a glaze of ice cracking around me.

"One minute I was yelling and tearing at the rope that held me in the boat, the next minute I was on land. I don't remember how I got out of the boat. I don't even remember beaching. My first memory is looking down the shore at the beached lifeboat and seeing it crumpled and split on a windswept point. The shore beside the jutting prow of a cliff was littered with life jackets and life rings, with oars and tanks, all sorts of flotsam, and with what looked like half a lifeboat, snapped in half by the waves that had humbled the *Big Fitz*. I turned around and walked back over the bare rock, bare because the wind had blown all the snow off. I retraced footsteps that seemed to be mine along a path through the woods to a small cabin. There was a fire going. I guess I had made it. My wetsuit was on the floor and the wrappings from my food bars on the table. I heard planes, and when I went out again ships seemed to be anchored offshore. I saw people looking around the flotsam and searching the beach.

"I crept along the treeline to hear what they were saying. I heard that twenty-nine men had been lost. I heard that there were no survivors. They obviously didn't know about me. The Captain had obviously been too busy with the storm to radio anyone about 'the stowaway,' me.

"The people searched the beach, but they didn't find the cabin or me."

"What about footprints? The smoke...."

"What? Oh, the footprints.... I just don't know. They didn't seem to see either the smoke or the footprints."

"Why didn't you go to them? They would want to know about you, a hero."

"Hero? Me? I jumped ship. I jumped ship when I had the opportunity to save twenty-nine men. I've walked this frozen shore now, for what? Two months? All my *thinks*, all my imaginings of me as hero are usurped by the picture of me scrambling up the side of that lifeboat, lashing myself to the seat just as the biggest wave of all rears up under the stern and plunges the bow to the bottom. Whether the lifeboat broke free when the *Fitz* hit bottom or whether it broke free from the force of the water, I don't know. Only I escaped, and I could have helped them all. Instead, I ran."

"Was there time? Time to warn them?"

"Uh?"

"You don't want to be a hero, to be successful.... Oh...."

"Clara? Clara? Are you all right? Clara! You look so awful, so sick. You're crying! I was so wound up in my story I didn't even notice you were getting sick. I just thought you were, well, ah, a bit of a tippler. Have you been sick all along? The pills? What can I do?"

"Get me a painkiller. And Gene, there's something else...."

"Brandy?"

"No. Would you help me to the outhouse?"

UNDATED · Dear Children: My house is in disorder. I am lying here on the couch. My clothes are filthy. I smell. I cannot wash. I cannot be bothered to wash. My standards are being eroded by pain. My brain is being eroded by painkillers. I have resorted to using the chamber. What ignominy! Someone else is going to have to empty it. There are few pretensions left, few dignities.

I am mustering my strength with a shot, a stiff shot, of brandy in order to talk to you.

A half-dead mouse is on the floor beside the couch. It was not killed outright and must have dragged itself over here. I can see it has gnawed the corner off the trap. Every once in a while it flutters to get free and then it lies still again. How I wish I could put it out of its misery. I just don't want to move.

I think it is morning. I have been on the couch for how long? I don't know what date it is. I believe it is February, a new month. The powdered milk I mixed days ago must be sour by now, the food bad, except for the provisions I stored for you in the root cellar.

After Gene left, there was a storm. The roof of the cottage cried. It cried in pain as the storm rained pellets of snow and branches onto it. The pressure of the wind must have been too much for the ice and a zigzag gash has opened up in the Lake. The water is dark and angry, trying to break free.

All seems quiet now. Could it possibly be peace? Oh, I don't want it to be peace yet. I have to get away from here.

Gene, where are you?

He was so kind to me last night. Was it last night? I went out to the loo—for the last time, I now realize—and I fell. Nothing new. I howled with pain and there was Gene, watching me. For the first time, I saw a shadow of concern in his eyes. He waited for me while I was in the loo, then we carefully walked back towards the cabin. Hanging on to his arm—I walk so stooped now—I told him of my plan, how he could help me. Do you know what he did? He left. He steadied me to the door of the cabin, went in and grabbed his belongings, and ran away. Now how can I get away from here? Is everything I have done so far going to be marred by him?

So far, I feel pretty good about what I have done, what I have said.

What if I'd been a lawyer, smart as I supposedly was? Would I have ever known what it was like to feel new life inside me, to participate in life's continuation? What a pity men can never know it. Would I have felt anything comparable to nurturing the lives that are the next generation, tomorrow's history? I feel satisfaction I have contributed.

I say contributed because I realize there are many other factors that have made you what you are today. A mother or a father can never take all the credit; your own individual strength—that unknown x-factor that allows some people to profit from bad experiences while others crumple, that allows some people to grow in a good environment while others are weakened by it—your own individual strength plays an unknown and yet important part.

Not that the job was easy. I was always so aware of what fragile blossoms your little lives were. Did I bruise you when I yelled at you? Did I expect too much of you? Was I too hard on you? I was so afraid of the mewling permissiveness of so many parents that seemed to be producing marshmallow adults. I was so afraid my own selfish individuality would come before you. I still remember the dream I had, Clarissa, when you were a toddler. I dreamed I was experiencing the lovely joys of making love only to find that you were almost strangled in your high chair.

When I left the house for the last time, I brought along with me the file marked "Children." I had filled it with mementoes of your growing up. The Mother's Day card you made for me, Andrew. "M is for Mother and for the million things you gave me." And the letters: remember your description of that barbaric hazing at university? Andrew. My son. And Clarissa. My daughter.

Your first drawings, as form gradually emerged from your random scribbling. And you gave up that talent as an artist to become an accountant! And remember that essay you wrote about how to talk to plants?

I want to be proud of my death, my last, perhaps only, really individual and free act.

Come on, Clara. Nobody knows what it is to be free. You may have come to terms with yourself. You may understand yourself better, but don't ever think you've solved the big problem of free will, of why you are doing what you are doing.

Shut up, mind.

Gene, where are you?

I waited to let him tell me his story and now he is gone and I am too weak to do anything. I lie here on the couch listening to the mouse struggle against its trap. What I would like to do is to get up and walk bravely through the snow to the special place way down the shore that I call the Turret, a place only I know about, although I have often offered to take you there. It has no memories for anyone, so nothing will be spoiled for you. But no matter how much motivation I have, my body will barely move.

Gene, where are you?

Do you realize you have jumped ship again? You jumped ship when you climbed trees to get away from your father, although it was your only solution. You jumped ship when you ran from your success in art. You jumped ship, not when you got into the lifeboat on the *Fitzgerald,* but when you hid from the searchers, jumping away from the recognition that you made a reasoned, correct choice.

Whatever could you do in the face of the storm? Not Lake Superior, but human.... For once, you jumped ship at the right time. But you can't admit it, can't accept you may have done the right thing, always want to feel like a bad little kid.

Now you've jumped ship when you again have the chance to do the right thing, to be honourable and helpful to me, to fulfill a promise. All I wanted you to do was to pull me on the toboggan down to the Turret, a long way, I realize. I did not tell you why—I don't want you to be legally implicated—but I think you may have guessed.

You can still change your mind and come back. If those hours of talking, of listening, if those painful hours of postponing my final peace did any good, you will come back. You still have time for a second chance.

I hear the storm mounting again. The Lake is cracking open. The wind is stacking the ice into sheaves of glass along the shore. The transparent Lake has become transparent glass, broken and stacked into neat sheaves.

I don't know how I will get water. But who needs water? I feel so light. I feel myself floating, no earthly body to give me pain, floating along the beach, floating over the transparent sheaves of ice, the wind mingling with my aerie spirit.

I won't say marvellous.

I don't need to.

The waves are huge now. Gene was right when he said they were like animals, huge frothing dragons rearing out of the sea.

Do you see that? Do you see that dragon rushing along the water, foam frothing from its crest? It is Mishipishu. There it goes. Rearing up. Why it is a she! I never before realized that. I'll bet the Indians didn't know that. There *she* goes, racing across the water, the wind tearing at *her* crest. Up *she* comes, rearing proudly above the waves, and then slowly, slowly submerging in a gurgle of bubbles.

Do you realize I am now blessed because Mishipishu has appeared to me? She is the most powerful manitou of all and she is now my spirit guardian.

Great Mishipishu, guardian of this mighty Lake, and of Clara, grant me my wish.

What is my wish?

Oh yes. I wish to remove my earthly body from this place. I

wish to keep this place sanctified for my children and their physical life here.

Whisk me down to my special place. There I will sit on the rocks, feel the spray on my face, drink a toast with this *eau de vie* as the welcome cold envelops me. I will join the memories of my children and my husband, memories of when we ran and danced on the beach, memories of when we loved and played and ate and laughed. I will join these memories and I will not be alone. We will never say goodbye.

Help me, Mishipishu. Help me get out of here.

I feel myself going down to the cave, the sacred place of the Indians. The pellets of snow are insinuating themselves into my eyes, my ears, my mouth. I am becoming part of the storm. By foot, it would be difficult going because of the glaze of ice on the beach. The agates are bright from the ice, polished by the sand and glazed by the waves, frozen into place as if time had stopped, which, of course, it never does. Or does it?

I am following my usual route to the cave, up over those bulging rocks and then around and down, wending my way through the corridors of lava, floating, floating. The gas holes in the lava are filled with copper and quartz, polka dots of beige and turquoise like the surface of a child's toy dog. Don't you believe me? Look the next time you are there.

The waves are thundering in. The Lake has broken free. As I approach the cave, the roar increases, the waves reverberating against the ice in the rock grotto, etching it deeper and deeper with each thrust, all snow drifts and icicles washed away. The surge almost touches the treeline, but never regularly. You would think you were safe to walk along the rocks as the waves diminish and lap and lap away at the shore. But then, without warning, one, two, three, they thrust up and over the ice, grabbing at the trees with their watery claws.

Chunks of ice are bobbing in the open water. Soon they will be massed together on the shore into voluptuous Henry Moore damsels; I love those shapes. The ice will turn a delicate turquoise blue. Then they will all break free from the shore and float to oblivion in the cobalt-blue water of Lake Superior, while the diamond tips of the ice-glazed trees nod and crackle in the wind.

Mishipishu, help me float to oblivion.

I can see my body on that couch, lying in its earthly mess. Old and hairy.

Remember me differently, Jeff. Remember me vibrant and young. And forgive yourself, if you need forgiving. I can't bear to think....

Oh, Mishipishu. Get me out of here. Help me get out of here.

§§§

"Clara. Clara. Are you all right? Wake up. I've come back. I will help you."

"Mishipishu?"

"Who? Clara, it's Gene."

"Gene?"

"I've been so wound up with my problems, with my unsettled state, I haven't been able to think of anything else. I haven't been able to see anything else. My god, how sick you are.

"Not until today have I been able to draw. Time and time again I tried to draw your face and I just couldn't remember it. Today I saw your face—and I saw your suffering. I became your suffering. And I could draw."

"Will you help me?"

"I will."

"Let me see your eyes."

"What? Are you raving?"

"Probably. But your eyes had the strangest look in them. A wild, unsettled look."

"Has it gone?"

"Yes."

"Well, do you want me to help you or not?"

"Oh, please, Gene. Please help me. I'm having such trouble getting up."

"Here, give me your hand."

"The snowshoes and toboggan are in the boathouse. You just have to pull me along the shore. What goes on there is my business. You don't know what that is, right?"

"Right."

"Please come back and clean up, will you? And empty the traps. And other things. I apologize for even asking you."

"That's okay. I'll do everything."

"But first, before we go, will you take this poor little mouse outside and put it out of its misery? It has been struggling for so long."

"I don't want to. But I will."

"Don't pick it up by the trap! Can't you see its leg is broken?"

"I'm sorry."

"Take it outside on that little shovel we use for the ashes. And give it a good whack on the head."

"Not a nice concept."

"Nice? At the price of a creature suffering?"

"All right. All right. Don't get excited."

"I know. I must save what strength I have."

"There. I've got it on the shovel".

"Good. While you go outside I'll just collect up my things.

"Let's see...."

There, he's gone.

Goodbye, my children. Goodbye, Jeff. Don't feel guilty. Don't. Not at least about what I am doing. This is my choice. By making this choice, I've come to terms with my life. Hopefully you can do the same.

Without qualification, knowing each of you for what you are, your good points and your bad, I can say with all my heart I love you. I know I have been remiss in not saying these words. I have instead tried to let my actions speak for me. I hope they have. I hope you have always known and felt that I love you.

Clarissa, come to terms with me. I understand why you have felt angry at me; don't feel guilty about it. Your Aunt Elizabeth felt so badly about rejecting all those loving outstretched arms of the family that she had to have psychotherapy after our first uncle died. I understand that your rejection of me was, at least in part, an inability to come to terms with me being sick. This is natural.

If only I had talked to you both like I have talked to you here. I cannot get over all the important—important to me, that is—all the thoughts I have had and never said to anyone. This undercurrent has been running through my life and I've never acknowledged it to anyone, or to myself.

I should have said more, communicated more, maybe even done more.

But I hope you agree my first job, my job of raising you, I did well. At least I have come to realize my importance there.

"Gene? Have you got everything ready?"

Goodbye, my loves.

"I looked after the mouse. And I found the toboggan and snowshoes."

"I've got the brandy. Now where's my purse?"

"Your purse?"

"Of course. Don't you know a woman can't go anywhere without her purse?"

"Clara, are you joking? Or raving again."

"Neither. But I need my purse. I have a backup in there. Just in case."

Intruders No More

"COME ON, TASHA. Let's go and see Nordri."

Maybe it will shake me out of the spell of Mother's journal. How I misjudged her. How I never let myself know her. She was quite a person.

Did she have some sort of unrecognized STD?

Old fuddy-dud Dad?

So many questions.

"Nordri didn't look very well when we went to see her yesterday. I hope she's okay. Her health, I mean. I never was worried about those creeps. Too scared."

Or were you too scared to drive down and check on her?

Never entered my head.

The snow had gone. The only reminder of it was a cascade of saplings still bowing over the road from the previous weight. An arched walkway had been created for Clarissa and her dog to walk through.

"Any more snow on those leaves and the laden branches would have broken the trees. Must be part of the reason leaves usually fall before the snow does."

So little smoke coming out of the chimney.

"Nordri?"

"Ah, missus. So good to see you. Come in. Come in."

Nordri was in a muu-muu, or shift, made out of fleece with hand embroidery on the edge of the sleeves and the neck. She wore felt slippers and strands of her fine white hair were wisping out from her ponytail in a sort of halo effect.

"You like good cuppa coffee, missus? I put on right way."

"No. Thanks. I just thought I'd walk down and see how you are."

"I fine."

"Everything all right, last night?"

"For sure. For sure. Yus fine."

"A lovely moon...."

"Good of you coming see me. I make some coffee. You stay. Yus a minute."

"Okay, I'll have coffee."

"Oh, I got no water, missus. Wait, I'm getting some."

"Here. Give me the pails. I'll get it."

Clarissa and her dog scrambled down the rough-hewn stairs winding through a stand of cedar gnarled and bent from the wind. On the beach, she could not stop her eyes from admiring the rocks, so big and polished from the waves, even the granite ones.

Like Thunder Bird eggs.

I said that, Mother, not you.

The Lake was sapphire blue, still gently rolling from the previous wind.

Harder to get water here without the potholes. Does she take off her shoes and wade in? No, she must climb out onto that little peninsula and dip the pail in there. Yes. Not easy, though.

Nordri was lying down on the quilt on her bed when Clarissa returned.

"You're not well?"

"I all right. Yus tired."

"Are you sure?"

"Sure I sure, missus."

"Here, I will make the coffee."

"That's nice. Everything right there. See that little mill there? A *sampo*. I find it here in cabin when cleaning. I give it you."

"It's beautiful. Are you sure?"

"Sure I sure."

"Thank you so much."

"Now I get coffee bread. It in tin. Maybe mice liking it. I put out egg for you. Maybe you not eat. See it there? Such wonderful shape. Like path of the world. The sun is yolk. The white is moon. It give life."

"Nordri, you are so positive."

"Alla time. It keep me going."

"Me? I would see the salmonella we've contaminated it with."

"Dat's true, too."

"I think I'll put some wood on the stove first, if you don't mind. It's getting chilly in here."

"Dat's good."

"You haven't got much wood, Nordri."

"I have enough. I know someplace where I'm getting some."

"I came to say goodbye. I'm leaving. After I see about a few repairs to the cottage."

"You leaving so soon, missus?"

"I have to go back to work."

"Too bad."

"I'll be back. In fact, our whole family will be starting to come back. My brother will bring his wife and kids. My dad will come. Well, I think my dad will come. I'll bring my friends."

"Dat's nice. When we talk earlier you not for sure."

"I know. I came here to see if we should sell the place or start using it again."

"You not selling?"

"No. Before, I never felt it was mine, but I do now."

"Dat's good."

"Are you leaving soon? If you are sick, you shouldn't stay here alone. I could help you pack up. Maybe call some of your family to help you?"

"No, missus. I all right. I stay here little bit longer. Then I leaving, too."

"I think I should take you out. Or maybe I should stay a little longer."

"No, missus. Respect me, please. Nordri needs no help."

"Well, after we have coffee, and your delicious *pulla*, and the egg, I'll go and get some wood for you."

"Okay, missus. It yus so nice to be here little while longer. Before I go."

Acknowledgements

ALWAYS I HAVE TO ACKNOWLEDGE the help of my husband, Stan Kurisko. He proofreads, makes suggestions, and gives moral support and encouragement. Captain Frank Prouse in Sault Ste. Marie helped me with the first edition. My publisher and editor, John Flood, suggested amplifying literary directions I barely saw. Dennis Choquette, proofreader, was ever-patient. Too, living beside the Lake where it could pulse through my being, living amongst humanity long enough to see its frailty, provided the stuff of my imagination.

Suggested Further Reading

Hugh E. Bishop, *The Night the Fitz Went Down,*
   (Duluth: Lake Superior Port Cities, 2000).

Joseph MacInnis, *Fitzgerald's Storm: The Wreck of the Edmund Fitzgerald,*
   (Toronto: Macmillan, 1997).

James R. Marshall, ed., *Shipwrecks of Lake Superior,*
   (Duluth: Lake Superior Port Cities, 1987).

Frederick Stonehouse, *The Wreck of the Edmund Fitzgerald,*
   (Gwinn: Avery Color Studios, 1998).

Julius F. Wolff Jr., *Lake Superior Shipwrecks,*
   (Duluth: Lake Superior Port Cities, 1990).

The Author

Novelist Joan Skelton was adamant about Toronto having no influence on her writing. Although born, raised, and educated exclusively in Toronto, Joan Skelton's spiritual home was not, and is not, there. She knew from childhood she would be a writer but it was not until she moved away from the large urban setting that she found her subject matter in the people and country of northern Ontario. GREG GATENBY, Toronto, A Literary Guide

JOAN SKELTON DIVIDES HER TIME between her main residence outside Thunder Bay on the leeward end of Lake Superior and her cottage outside Sault Ste. Marie on the windward end. Her vocations have been writing and family; her avocations photography and dogs. An important interest reflected in her books and freelance articles has always been the human relationship to the natural world.

THE SURVIVOR OF THE EDMUND FITZGERALD
Joan Skelton

Second edition | First printing

The Survivor of the Edmund Fitzgerald was set in Perpetua
(12½ / 15) and Joanna Italic by Dennis Choquette. Both type-
faces were designed by Eric Gill and issued in digital form by
Monotype. The text stock is Domtar Plainfield, an acid-free,
Forestry Stewardship Council-certified paper milled in Port
Edwards, Wisconsin. The cover stock is Domtar Proterra.